Theft: And Other Tales of Loss and the Working Class

By John Abbott

Underground Voices
Los Angeles, California
2015

Published by Underground Voices
www.undergroundvoices.com
ISBN: 978-0692406540

For Sarah and Jillian.
Thank you for all the love and support.

CONTENTS

THEFT

The burglar didn't get much: his wallet, her purse, some change left on the counter, and a bag of cookies someone had forgotten to put away. The policeman, a young guy who lived in their neighborhood, made some sort of joke about crooks needing late night snacks too. Devon laughed. Alexis, his wife, looked at them both and then cleared her throat.

"How did he get in?" she said.

The policeman seemed ready to laugh again and he bit down on his lip once before answering her.

"He used your ladder," he said. "Climbed right up it and went through a window. I figure he left the same way. That's probably why he didn't take anything large like the television."

Devon felt heat all over his face and he wondered if he was sweating too. He looked away from his wife. Yesterday afternoon he had been cleaning the gutters — they had gotten so bad a row of plants had shot up — and he stopped near the end to get a drink of water. He was so hot he had decided to finish up later but never got around to it.

"Did you have much in your wallet and purse?" the policeman said.

They told him that besides their driver's licenses there was just a little cash, maybe twenty dollars between the two of them.

"I'd wait a day or two before getting a new license," he said. "Mrs. Hanlon down the street was broken into last month but she found her purse the next day. It was in her back yard. She saw it when she was watering her rose bushes."

The policeman flipped his notebook shut, said he'd be in touch, and headed for the front door, stepping over their son's toys on the way. Before he left, Alexis asked him about their bicycles that had been stolen the week before. The bicycles getting stolen had been Devon's fault too. Neither of them had mentioned the bikes since then and the atmosphere in the house seemed to change when she brought them up; Devon couldn't look at anything or anyone for more than a second. The officer shifted his weight a couple times before speaking.

"That wasn't my case," he said. "I'll have someone call you."

After he was gone they stood in the kitchen, neither one of them speaking. She seemed to be staring at a section of the counter, studying it as if there was a stain and she couldn't remember how it got there. He poured himself a second cup of coffee and straightened his tie.

"Well," he said. "I guess I should be getting to work."

She nodded. He kissed her goodbye, whispering, "I'm sorry," as he drew away from her. He didn't turn around to see her reaction and he told himself it was because he was already running late. Once he was in the car it occurred to him that he didn't know exactly what he had apologized for.

Devon found a note on the kitchen counter when he got home from work. Benny and I went to stay at my sister's for the air conditioning. Will call later. Love, Alexis. The writing, even where she had written her name, looked like it had been scribbled down in a hurry. Before loosening his tie or taking off his shoes, he dialed his sister in-law's phone number. The phone rang and rang. He tapped his foot and twisted the cord in his hands. After what seemed like a million rings the answering machine beeped on. The beep took him by surprise. He had no idea what he was going to say. Finally, he mumbled something about going for a beer with a friend from work. He said he wouldn't be gone longer than an hour and hung up the phone.

He fumbled around the kitchen for a while, opening the fridge and looking through cupboards before deciding he wasn't hungry. Lately he hadn't felt much like eating. Neither had Alexis. Both of them blamed the recent heat wave. For two weeks now it hadn't rained and the temperature during the day was never lower than ninety. Every night one of them still fixed dinner — they traded off cooking duty — and they sat at the dining room table with their son, Benny. They watched as he ate all the food in front of him, talking excitedly in between each bite. It didn't seem like that long ago since getting him to eat even half of his food was a chore. This memory, when they spoke of it after dinner, was one of the few things that still could make them both smile.

The bar was already crowded when he got there. Lately it seemed like the bars filled up earlier and earlier each night. Even though the place wasn't very big it took him a while to find Mitch. He found him at the far end of the place, leaning against a wall, beer in one hand.

"Hey," Mitch said. "I'm trying to get us a pool table but there's already six people ahead of us."

Mitch drank some of his beer, wiped foam off his lips, and looked around the room.

"It's like every shoprat in town is here."

The way he said shoprat was like a curse except he kept his voice low so no one around would hear. A while back Devon managed to work into conversation the fact that his father had been an autoworker, figuring Mitch would pick up the hint. He never did though.

Devon ordered a beer, declined the bartender's offer to start a tab, and took his drink back to where Mitch was waiting. There still weren't any pool tables open. They stood against the back wall, drinking their beers, occasionally talking but mostly watching the crowd.

"Alexis let you out for the night?" Mitch said.

9

Devon looked away from him and drank some of his beer. He hated when Mitch talked in stereotypes. At work it was the same thing. He spoke about management as though they were all one person even though a couple of them were pretty decent.

"Actually," Devon said. "She took Benny over to her sister's."

"You really are a free man. Me, I got the opposite problem. An ex-girlfriend came to stay last night. She got canned and had to move out of her apartment. I kind of owe her some money so I couldn't turn her down."

Mitch reached into his pocket and came out with a pack of cigarettes.

"I haven't had one of these in days. Then Sherri comes to stay and walks around my place in her underwear because she can't stand to be hot. I smoked half a pack last night."

Devon laughed, mainly because he thought it was expected.

"Something's gotta break though," he said. "I can't deal with that over and over till she finds her own place."

Devon was about to tell Mitch what he had been thinking ever since he came home from work and saw Alexis's note; she thought he couldn't protect his family and that was why she went to stay at her sister's. The words were halfway out of his mouth when one of the guys playing pool signaled that it was their turn. Mitch crushed out his cigarette and accepted the cue stick from the other guy.

Their game didn't last long. Devon couldn't focus on any of his shots; he should have just said what was on his mind. Afterwards they talked for a few minutes over a second beer. He still thought about saying something — despite his other faults Mitch always listened to his problems — but really he knew there was more to the situation than bikes or the break-in last night. He and Alexis hadn't been getting along for a while now. They snapped at each other for no apparent reason and afterward the apologies seemed to come harder. He wanted to tell Mitch all of this and more but he knew it would require a good deal of time and at least a few more beers. And because he wanted to stay clearheaded for when Alexis came back he declined Mitch's offer to stay and shoot another game when their turn came around again. They finished their beers, said goodbye, and went their separate ways. On the short walk home — it was only four blocks — he did nothing but worry. Did he miss Alexis's call while he was out? Had he locked all the windows?

The inside of the house was sticky and hot and he felt like he needed a cold shower and another change of clothes. First, though, he checked the answering machine. No messages. He picked up the phone, held it to his ear, and listened for the dial tone. After making sure it worked he set the phone down and went upstairs. He took a long time showering and changing and laying out his work clothes for the next day. He also spent a while in Benny's room, picking up toys and folding some laundry that Alexis had done earlier. Performing these routine jobs helped him relax. When he couldn't think of anything else to do upstairs he went down to the sofa, placed the phone nearby, and lay down. He turned the T.V. on for background noise and closed his eyes.

He woke up to the phone ringing. Outside the windows the sky was a dark gray tinged with yellow like it might storm soon. His eyes took a minute to adjust to the failing light and his voice was thick when he said hello. Alexis said hello and asked him how work was.

"Fine," he said. "It's getting late. Aren't you and Benny coming home?"

He heard a rustling on the other end of the line. Then someone's voice.

11

"Sorry, I thought I wrote that we were staying here tonight. It's just too hot at our house."

He thought he heard her voice change pitch but he couldn't be sure; there were even more noises on her end now, one of them he recognized as his son's voice.

"Here," she said. "I'll put Benny on so you can say good night."

Before he could even decide to ask if he should come by she was handing over the phone. Benny sounded very tired and didn't say much besides the fact that Aunt Theresa had taken them out for ice cream. They exchanged good nights and said I love you. Devon waited to see if Alexis would come back on the line but within a minute he heard the receiver click. He sat up quickly and threw the phone against the couch cushions. His head felt all stuffy from sleeping, his two beers, and most of all, confusion. He couldn't understand why Alexis hadn't even invited him. True, he didn't care much for his sister in-law, Theresa, but they rarely fought or argued, especially in the last seven years, since Benny had been born.

He turned off the television and stalked around the house, first the living room, then the kitchen. For a moment he considered having a drink, something strong like the whisky his father in-law gave them every year for their anniversary because he said it was important to have good liquor around for when company showed up. He opened the high cupboard, the one above the refrigerator, stood on his tiptoes, but couldn't reach the bottle. The whisky must have gotten pushed back some. Now he would need a stepstool if he wanted to get it down. He decided it would be too much trouble and returned to the living room couch. The T.V. was showing the news. The weather report said there was no sign of the heat letting up, not for weeks anyway.

Devon watched the rest of the news and some of an old detective movie before going upstairs. As he entered the near dark of the bedroom he had a fleeting sense that Alexis was in the room, perhaps straightening up the closet, and that in a moment he would see her slip off her nightgown before climbing into bed. The tension of his thought left him standing in the doorway for several minutes. When he spoke her name out loud, mostly just to shatter the spell that seemed to lie over the room, he realized he couldn't remember the last time they had spent the night apart. He took a long time undressing and getting into bed and even before he had fully laid his head on the pillow he knew he wouldn't sleep. Everything about the bed seemed different: its weight, softness, even its smell. His pulse was off too, every heartbeat seemed irregular, not to mention loud. But still he tried to sleep, shutting his eyes and taking deep breaths in an attempt to calm himself. Two hours later he was still awake. He regretted falling asleep on the couch, earlier. Finally, after counting up the hours he had till it was time for work he decided to take a couple allergy pills that usually made him drowsy. He swallowed the pills along with a small glass of water. Afterwards he lay down on the couch, planning to stay there just until he felt tired enough; but in the morning he woke up to the first light creeping through the living room blinds. The first thing he did was reach out for the warm body that was usually lying next to him.

The phone rang as Devon tried to force down a breakfast of toast and coffee. He picked up the phone and his heart sped up a little when he heard Alexis's voice.

"I'm glad you picked up," she said. "I was hoping I'd catch you before you left for work."

He thought her voice sounded tired and he wondered if she hadn't slept well either.

"I was thinking maybe after you get off work we could take Benny to the lake?"

"Yeah," he said. "I'll bring my suit along and swing by as soon as I'm done."

He was smiling now and eager to end the conversation before anything unpleasant came up.

"I'll tell Benny," she said. "He'll be looking forward to it."

They exchanged goodbyes and he hung up the phone. He hurried upstairs, grabbed his swimsuit, and left the house without finishing the coffee or toast.

At work he was in a good mood. He breezed through all his assignments and drank lots of coffee to help make up for a bad night's sleep — the allergy pills for whatever reason usually gave him strange dreams, like the one he had last night where he was climbing a ladder while underwater. Even Mitch's constant chatter about his ex-girlfriend didn't bother him much. Whenever his work didn't require too much concentration he thought about going to the beach later on; playing in the water with Benny, buying him popsicles from the concession stand, rubbing sunscreen on Alexis's shoulders and back.

After lunch he returned to his desk and saw that he had a message from the policeman handling the burglary case. The message was short. The man said they were pretty sure they had found his wallet. All he needed to do was come down to the station to identify it and then he could have it back. He thought about leaving early but one of the managers had dumped a new pile of work on his desk over the lunch break. There was no way he would finish before five o'clock. He tried though: drinking more coffee even though he didn't usually have any in the afternoon and putting on the glasses he rarely wore so that his eyes didn't tire. He was so lost in the stack of papers he almost didn't notice when it was quitting time.

The trip to the station didn't take long. He identified his wallet, signed some papers, and was done. But the traffic was bad and he arrived at Theresa's almost an hour late. When he saw Alexis the first words out of her mouth were, "Where were you?" He explained why he was late and how a police officer had found his wallet in the dumpster located in the park down the street.

"You could have called," she said. "Benny's been waiting."

"Well I'm here now if you're ready to go."

Alexis scratched at a mosquito bite on her arm, set her hands on her hips, and shook her head.

"Why don't you just take Benny?" she said. "I've got some stuff to do around here."

They didn't stay long at the lake. The heat felt crushing and the lake was like bathwater. During their favorite game — Devon tossing Benny in the air so that he splashed into the water — it seemed like something was different. After every toss Benny would say, "You're not doing it right, dad."

"You're right," Devon said. "I'm not throwing you high enough. I'll do better this time." But Benny just looked at him and said, "That's not it."

The only moment when Devon felt at ease was when he watched Benny suck down two red, white, and blue popsicles. Afterward they changed back into their clothes and drove to Theresa's. When they came in the house Theresa and Alexis were watching television and drinking tall glasses of pink lemonade. Theresa announced that she made sandwiches for everyone. Benny hurried into the kitchen, saying hi to his mom and aunt as he ran.

"I guess I'll stick around for a little," Devon said. "And then we can all go home."

"I was actually thinking about staying another night," Alexis said. "It's even hotter today than yesterday."

Devon watched as Theresa raised her glass to her lips. He thought she did it to hide a smile. Alexis set her drink on a coaster, rose to her feet, and moved across the room till she was standing next to him. She seemed to walk slowly and with an exaggerated swaying of her hips.

15

"You're welcome to stay too," she said. "Theresa said it'd be fine."

She spoke as if Theresa wasn't in the room. He moved so that his back was now to his sister in-law.

"Look, Alexis," he said, keeping his voice low and calm. "I know things have been bad since the bikes got stolen and then I left the ladder out but nothing else is going to happen. You should come home."

He stopped talking and waited for her reply. He was looking so intently at her closed lips that it surprised him to hear a voice.

"She doesn't blame you, Devon," It was Theresa talking. He turned to face her.

"I'm talking to my wife here," he said.

His voice rose and turned sharp without his meaning to. Alexis shook her head and said his name. He saw in her eyes the same look of frustration she usually reserved for Benny. He was already sweating under his arms and on his forehead but now his whole body felt wet, like he hadn't properly dried off at the lake. His hands seemed to move on their own and he had to cross his arms to keep from pointing at her — she hated when he did that. Probably he would have smashed something like the lemonade glasses on the table if they had been within his reach.

"This is all bullshit!" he said. "We don't even have that much and people are stealing from us. They should be breaking into houses in your parents' neighborhood."

As he spoke he realized these thoughts had been bouncing around the corner of his mind for over a week now.

"You should go, honey," Alexis said. "I'll call you tomorrow."

He nodded, staring at her as he regained his breath. She looked both older and younger at the same time. He had the strange feeling that if he looked at Theresa and then back at his wife they would appear as the same person. He nodded once more and left the house, careful not to look into the next room where he was sure their son was standing in the doorway, sandwich in hand, watching his parents fight.

He didn't even try the bed that night. He came home well past dark, tired from endless driving. For the first hour after leaving Theresa's he drove because the thought of his empty house was too much. He toyed with the idea of calling Mitch to see if he could stay there but he quickly remembered that he already had a guest. Alexis's parents were his only other option and, under the current circumstances, he didn't think he should even bother. So he kept driving and kept the windows rolled down so the rush of the wind would clear his mind.

When he got back, the night air had cooled his sweat but not the itching thirst he had. He got out a step stool, fetched the whisky bottle from its place in the top cupboard, and drank. After two large gulps he replaced the bottle. He shut the cupboard but left out the step stool, just in case. It turned out to be a good thing; after making sure the house was locked up he had a few more swigs before stripping out of his clothes, turning on the television for background noise, and making himself as comfortable as he could on the couch.

He woke to a harsh scraping noise; metal against metal perhaps. At first he thought it was only something on the television but when he looked up only a man and woman were on the screen, talking to each other as they held hands. He got up from the couch and pulled back some of the curtain. Through the window he saw something move outside in the middle of the street. His eyes were still blurry and he thought the dark object was probably a nocturnal animal like a raccoon. The scraping sound continued and, after rubbing his eyes, Devon could focus better, enough to see that it wasn't an animal at all. It was a manhole cover being pushed to the side; a man's head popped up through the opening. Immediately, he knew he should call the police; someone climbing out of a manhole in the middle of the night couldn't mean anything good.

But he didn't move and he wasn't quite sure why. Part of it was the strangeness of the scene he was watching; now the man was dragging the manhole cover to the curb. And then there was the feeling that if another intruder tried breaking into his house he would handle it himself. He wasn't sure what that meant exactly but he liked the sound of it. A list of household items he could use as weapons came to mind: kitchen knives, wrenches, hammers, his son's baseball bat.

Outside, a car pulled up to the curb and Devon watched what happened next like he was in a trance; the driver popped the trunk, climbed out of the car, and helped the other man lift the manhole cover into the trunk. They drove off; and by the time he thought to get the license plate numbers the car was too far away, he couldn't make anything out. He stood there for a while, debating if he should still call the police. He eventually decided the story was too unbelievable — he wasn't even sure he believed it, after all, he had gotten a little drunk — and went back to the couch, hoping he would be able to fall asleep again.

The heat wave didn't let up for two weeks. People stayed indoors whenever they could, watching movies they wouldn't ordinarily see and hanging out with people they weren't really friends with so long as they had air conditioning. Gas prices went up. The crime rate jumped; people reported an alarming number of burglaries; manhole covers across the city were swiped and sold for scrap metal. In two weeks the city saw five people murdered. Police officers frequently worked double shifts to keep up with the work. A few days after the police found Devon's wallet a neighborhood woman found Alexis's purse tangled in her dried up rhododendron bushes. The woman had been on vacation which is why she didn't find the purse sooner.

Devon called Alexis at Theresa's to tell her the news and she replied that she had bought a new purse the other day. Both of them were quiet for a while. He couldn't think of anything to say except for the incident about the manhole cover so he waited for her to speak first. She began telling him about everything she and Benny had done in the past couple days and how much he missed his dad. In the middle of her talk she stopped abruptly and he could hear her sigh into the receiver.

"We need to talk sometime soon," she said.

He let the pause build for a moment before replying, "I know."

They met at a restaurant, neutral territory. He was a little nervous and had a couple sips of whisky before showing up. The meeting went well though. She admitted something had gone wrong between them only she didn't know quite what it was. They talked about all the possibilities and couldn't settle on anything

"Maybe it's just a phase," she said. "I'm sure all married couples go through them once in a while."

He nodded and poked at his food, wondering if he looked as ragged to her as he looked to himself. At night he couldn't sleep unless he took pills or drank.

"I think I just need a little more time," she said. "Unless you think it would be best for us if I came back now?"

He wanted her back, in large part because he knew she would help him pull himself together. But he understood that she was only being polite with her offer.

"Take as much time as you need," he said, putting down his fork and picking up the beer he had ordered.

And she did take her time. Two more weeks passed before she would return home; although they saw each other frequently. They even made love once, taking advantage of a night when Theresa took Benny to a movie. Judging by their awkwardness and lack of tenderness, Devon understood it would take a long time for them to work out their troubles, whatever they were. Every day seemed to pass slower, although he didn't mind so much because they didn't even compare to his insomniac nights. He had taken up the habit of calling Mitch and the two of them met at the bar. Mitch informed him that he and his ex-girlfriend were screwing again but they didn't sleep together.

"It's the best of everything," he said.

Their usual bar seemed completely different late at night. The jukebox played incessantly and people that Devon had never seen before danced and drank all through the night, stopping only to cool off for a moment. He never took part, although he had been asked to dance by a couple different women. He preferred to sit by himself in one of the corners; drinking, staring at the T.V. screen, and occasionally nodding off in the best sleep he was able to get those days. When Mitch was ready to leave he usually had to wake Devon up and drag him by the arm through the bar and out into the street. On the night before Alexis's return Devon got drunker than usual and Mitch needed the help of the woman he was leaving with — he was going to her house — to get him outside.

A sound like gunshots split the night air. Devon snapped awake, his eyes wide open and looking all around like someone was after him. Mitch laughed and slapped him on the back.

"It's O.K.," he said. "It's just fireworks."

Mitch leaned over and kissed the woman from the bar.

"Yeah," she said. "It's a celebration."

He nodded, but through the fog of confusion and drink he couldn't figure out what exactly they meant.

THE KING

Reggie was playing the radio again. He sat with the old transistor on his lap, one hand resting on the top like he was petting a small animal. The radio played old rock and roll songs and he tapped along to the rhythm. He sat in the middle of the garage on the cold concrete floor. The garage smelled like cigarettes, not the ones his mom smoked but the kind his older brother smoked, the ones that didn't come in a pack which meant his brother or one of his friends had to roll them. He looked out across the street toward the carved pumpkins glowing a spooky orange. Mr. Lecrone lived at that house and earlier in the day he had let him carve a pumpkin, watching carefully over his shoulder as he struggled to shape the teeth with the orange handled safety knife. "Take er' easy now," Mr. Lecrone had said. "The teeth are the most important part." When he finished carving, Mr. Lecrone gave him a thumbs up and told him he was a natural. Reggie liked the pointed teeth and thought they looked scary, like a vampire's fangs. His fingers still smelled from scooping out the pumpkin guts. He liked the smell and every few minutes he stopped tapping and brought his fingers to his nose.

A song by Elvis came on the radio and he thought about getting up to dance in his costume. His aunt had made the rhinestone suit for him when she came home from art school last weekend. After she finished she had him try it on.

"You're even more handsome than Elvis," she had said. "Now let me see you shake those hips."

He wished his aunt still lived with them instead of with her new husband. If she were here she could take him trick or treating. Earlier in the day his mom had promised to take him but that was before Paul, her boyfriend, came over. When he reminded her of her promise she had told him to go along with his older brother Jesse.

He didn't want to tell his mom that Jesse didn't really go trick or treating. Jesse and his friends went around and stole candy from the younger kids.

"Why can't I go by myself?" Reggie had said.

"Are you kidding," his mom said. "Have you seen the kind of people that live in this neighborhood?"

The Elvis song ended and the station went to a commercial. Reggie stood up and brushed dirt off the backside of his costume. He decided he would ask Mom once more if she would take him trick or treating. She always told him not to bother her when her boyfriend was over but he had a plan. He knew his Mom and Paul would probably run out of beer soon. The party store they bought their beer from was a few blocks away. They could take him along and he'd at least get to a few houses and show people his costume.

Reggie shut off the radio. He set it down on one of the wooden shelves near the front of the garage. Outside the garage it was cool and smelled like dead leaves. He walked up to the back of his house, stopping at the back door. He went inside. The back door opened up to a little mud room. He carefully took off the blue suede shoes his aunt had found for him at a local costume store. Beyond the mud room was the kitchen. The kitchen smelled like ketchup, French fries, beer, and the hamburgers his mom had cooked for dinner. On the counter Reggie saw a whole bunch of empty beer cans: blue ones with a red leaf, and gold ones with white letters, and white ones with blue letters. He smiled, feeling pretty sure his plan would work.

The swinging door that opened up to the living room was closed. Reggie pushed it open a little. The room was dark except for the light he was letting in from the kitchen. He stopped when he saw his Mom and Paul on the couch. They were naked. He was on top of her, his butt going up and down real fast. Reggie let go of the door and it swung shut. He walked out of the kitchen slowly, trying not to make any noise. He picked up his shoes from the mud room and took them back to the garage.

Reggie took the radio out of its hiding place. He turned it on, hoping to hear something good like maybe the Monster Mash or Elvis but instead it was a love song, a really slow one. He sat down on the floor with the radio. He put the radio in his lap and one hand on the dial. He turned the dial slowly, playing a game he liked where he tried to find new stations, strange ones buried mostly in static but still there. He liked to imagine that they were radio stations in far away cities, cities he had heard of but never seen like St. Louis, Memphis, and Chicago, where Reggie's Dad had gone to live.

He kept turning the dial but none of the stations were coming in. All he could hear was static and an occasional voice that sounded like someone trying to talk underwater. He went back to his rock and roll station and thought about playing a different game, one he and Jesse used to play. Each time a song came on they would take turns trying to guess the title and the band. Reggie tried playing for a couple songs but it was no fun unless someone was there to hear you guess right.

Across the street he saw a group of trick or treaters walking up to Mr. Lecrone's house. There was a princess, a gorilla, a ghost, and two vampires; one with a black cape and the other a red one. They were all laughing and swinging their pillowcases full of candy. He watched them ring the doorbell. Mr. Lecrone came out holding a big dish. Reggie imagined it was full of miniature Snickers bars and peanut butter cups. Mr. Lecrone always had good candy. He heard the kids all say "Trick or Treat!" They held open their pillowcases and Mr. Lecrone put what looked like three or four pieces of candy in each one. Once the kids had their candy they took off down the sidewalk, their feet crunching up dry leaves as they ran.

Reggie got up and put his radio in its hiding place. He took a step outside of the garage, looked back toward his house then ran across the street. He stopped at a big pile of leaves next to the woodpile at the edge of Mr. Lecrone's yard. The woodpile had always seemed huge, about twice as big as he was, but the pile of leaves was even bigger. He wanted to climb onto the wood and jump into the leaves, get lost in their smell and the crackling sound they'd make. He thought about it for a while then decided it would ruin the costume his aunt had made. He was pretty sure he wasn't going to trick or treat tonight but he didn't want to hurt his aunt's feelings.

Another group of trick or treaters was coming up to Mr. Lecrone's. This time it was a robot, a soldier, and a ninja with a really neat looking sword on his back. They were taller than he was and probably older. He wondered if they would say yes if he asked if he could tag along. The idea seemed like a good one until he thought about his mom. If she found out he would probably get in trouble. It would be like the time he tried to clean the house for her when she was sick and he accidentally messed up the T.V. by spraying too much Windex.

"Oh, Reggie," she had said, taking the bottle from his hands.

Reggie hid behind the leaves until the trick or treaters passed. When the sound of their laughter was far away he came out. He didn't know why he hid behind the leaves exactly. He just knew he didn't want those kids to see him. They might have thought someone had stolen his candy since he didn't even have a bag.

He walked up to Mr. Lecrone's door and rang the bell. Mr. Lecrone opened the door holding the candy dish with both hands.

"Well look what we have here," he said.

Mr. Lecrone curled his lip and sang a few lines of 'Hound Dog'. Reggie didn't think Mr. Lecrone sounded anything like Elvis. His voice was too quiet and scratchy but he liked to hear him sing anyway.

"Here," Mr. Lecrone said, holding out the candy dish. "Take as much as you want."

In the dish there was everything that Reggie had imagined. The Snickers bars were big size instead of mini and there were also Milky Way and Baby Ruths. Reggie took one peanut butter cup, opened the wrapping, and popped it into his mouth. He chewed the candy, letting the creamy peanut butter coat his tongue.

"Where's your bag?" Mr. Lecrone said.

He said he didn't have one.

"Aren't you trick or treating?"

He shook his head.

"Why not? You've got your costume on and everything."

Reggie turned his head, looked across the street at his house then looked down at his shoes.

"Why don't you stay here," Mr. Lecrone said. "You can help me pass out candy."

Reggie liked passing out the candy. He liked how Mr. Lecrone let him hold the big bowl and drop as much candy into each bag as he wanted.

"Don't be stingy," he had said. "I've got plenty more in the kitchen."

He tried to give each boy or girl the same amount but sometimes he saw a really cool costume like a zombie dripping blood and pus and then he'd give them an extra peanut butter cup.

In between trick or treaters they waited inside. Reggie would have liked to watch a monster movie or something on T.V. but Mr. Lecrone didn't have one. He said he liked hobbies that make you think, like chess. Reggie liked chess too; he liked to move the carved wooden pieces around the board, form them into armies, or play farm with the pieces that looked like horses.

"That one's the knight," Mr. Lecrone would say, pointing to the piece Reggie was moving around. "And that one's the bishop."

Reggie could usually remember most of them except for the rook; he still called it the castle. He was playing with the castles, stacking them up to make a larger castle, when the doorbell rang.

"That's us, Reggie," Mr. Lecrone said.

Reggie grabbed the candy dish on the way to the front door. He opened the door and saw two kids. Both of them were taller than his brother. They each wore blue jeans and a t-shirt. One of them, the taller one, also had on a gold necklace. They both smelled like the cigarettes his brother smoked.

"Aren't you fellas too old for Halloween?" Mr. Lecrone said.

"We're only fifteen," the boy with the necklace said.

"Yeah," the other boy said. "We're just tall for our age."

The boys turned to each other and laughed. They each held out a bag toward Reggie.

"Where's your costume then?" Mr. Lecrone said.

The boy with the necklace took a toothpick from his pocket. He shoved the toothpick into the side of his mouth and then spoke.

"We're hoboes," he said.

"Yeah," the other one said. "Just a couple folks down on their luck."

Reggie looked up at Mr. Lecrone. His jaw was moving up and down like he had stuffed his mouth full of gum. The two boys had big smiles, bigger, it seemed to Reggie, than the glowing pumpkins and their crooked teeth.

"Give them a piece," Mr. Lecrone said.

Reggie dug his hand into the dish. He wasn't paying attention to what kind of candy he grabbed like he usually did. He thought he took out two pieces though he wasn't sure. He stared at the shadows the pumpkins made on the porch as he dropped the candy into each bag.

"There," Mr. Lecrone said. "Now thank the boy and move on."

The taller boy flicked the toothpick side to side with his tongue.

"We need some more," he said.

"Remember," the other boy said. "We're down on our luck."

"Give them one more Reggie," Mr. Lecrone said. "Then we're going inside."

Reggie thought his voice sounded even scratchier than it did earlier when he was singing Elvis. He grabbed as much candy as he could hold and gave it to the boys. He kept staring at the shadows, their shapes flickering wildly as the wind blew.

"How about you just give us all of it," the taller boy said, taking the toothpick out of his mouth.

Reggie looked up quick and saw the boy wasn't smiling. Mr. Lecrone bent down and whispered in Reggie's ear.

"Take the candy and go inside."

The shorter boy reached out and snatched the bowl from Reggie. Reggie felt a hand pushing him inside. He was pushed so hard he fell over but he managed to get his hands on the ground before hitting his face. Once inside he turned around to see what was happening. He saw Mr. Lecrone grab the taller boy's shirt by the neck.

"You niggers get off my porch," Mr. Lecrone said. "Before I break your skinny little asses."

Mr. Lecrone let go of the boy's shirt. The boy smiled and flicked his toothpick into the grass.

"That's fine, old man," he said. "We'll go. But from now on you best watch your ass."

Reggie moved the chess pieces around the board, dragging them really, with no specific game in mind. Mr.

Lecrone sat across from him with his head bent down and his hands squeezed together. It looked to Reggie like he was going to say something. His mouth opened then he shut it and moved his jaw up and down.

"You want some candy?" Mr. Lecrone said. "There's more in the kitchen."

Reggie shook his head. He thought about the word Mr. Lecrone had yelled at the boys. He knew it was a bad thing to say. He had heard his Mom tell Paul not to use it. "You want the boy to hear?" she'd say.

"You feel the same way I do," Paul had said. "You just don't say it out loud and that makes you think you're better somehow."

Reggie stopped playing with the pieces. He tried to put them back in their right places like he had seen Mr. Lecrone do but it was hard to remember.

"You can leave them how they are," Mr. Lecrone said.

He nodded.

"I think I have some Elvis records downstairs," Mr. Lecrone said. "You want me to look?"

"I think maybe I should go home," Reggie said.

Mr. Lecrone nodded.

The lights were on in the living room when Reggie crossed the street to come home. He hoped that meant his Mom and Paul were done being naked. The wind was blowing leaves through the street and Reggie felt cold in his costume. He thought about his bed, the warm blankets, and the flannel pajamas his aunt gave him last year for his birthday. He came into the house through the back door, took his shoes off, and walked into the warm kitchen. He went toward the living room door, planning to go right upstairs. He stopped when he heard someone talk.

"Why are you getting up?"

His Mom sounded sleepy or sad, he wasn't sure.

"I told you I wasn't staying the night."

"Please, could you?"

"You've got the kids tonight."

"I always have them."

Reggie backed away from the door in case someone was going to come into the kitchen. He thought about going down to the basement and then decided it would be too cold.

"If I stay," Paul said. "They'll just get used to seeing me around. They might start expecting things of me like I was their daddy."

Reggie remembered what Jesse had told him after their Dad left and then again when Mom started dating. "You only get one Dad," Jesse had said. "Just one little brother and he's gone for good."

"Paul," his mom said. "Just one night. You can leave early and the kids won't even know."

"I'll call you," he said.

Reggie ran to the basement. He didn't want to go down there but he didn't want Paul to see him. Paul could be nice sometimes like when he let Reggie scratch the lotto tickets he bought from the party store but mostly he smelled like beer and said lots of bad words to him and his mom.

The light was on in the laundry room, one bare bulb hanging above the washer. He stood underneath the bulb, looking at the piles of clothes on the floor. One of the piles was big enough to jump on, not as big as the leaf pile across the street but still big. He saw one of his brother's sweatshirts on top of the pile. The basement was colder than upstairs and the sweatshirt looked warm. It was too big and it smelled sweaty but he put it on anyway. He moved closer to the stairs and listened until he heard Paul leave through the back door.

His mom was crying. He could hear her even though he was in the kitchen and even though she had turned on the T.V. — the picture still faded out now and then from the time he sprayed it with Windex — and even though outside a group of trick or treaters were laughing and crunching through the leaves. He thought he should go to her, maybe make her feel better somehow, do his Elvis dance for her maybe. He knew she would reach out to him, hug him tight and say, "You're my boy, ain't you my boy," and he would nod and she would smile. But he knew her breath probably smelled like beer. He hated that smell. If he smelled it for too long he knew he would puke and then she'd get mad at him for messing up the living room carpet. He decided he would go to the garage. He would listen to the radio for a while till Mom went to bed. Then he could go to his room, get into his flannel pajamas, dive under all his blankets, and curl up tight.

The lights at Mr. Lecrone's house were still on. The pumpkins were still glowing too. He watched them from his spot in the garage. He remembered how last year all the pumpkins disappeared from porches the day after Halloween and ended up in pieces all over the neighborhood. Every sidewalk in the neighborhood was strewn with rotten orange chunks, shriveled up seeds and sometimes even a piece of the stalk. He had a feeling Jesse and his friends snuck out late and smashed them all. Reggie knew it was a mean thing to do but he thought it would be fun to see the pumpkin break into pieces and the seeds fly everywhere.

The air outside the garage smelled like cigarettes again, the ones Jesse smoked. He heard some people talking and it sounded like they were coming toward the garage. He turned his radio off to hear them better. It was probably Jesse and his friends but it could have been the boys from Mr. Lecrone's house and that scared him a little. He stood up and looked around for a good hiding spot just in case. The garage was mostly empty except for a lawnmower, a watering can, some old rusty tools his dad had left behind, and in one corner choked with cobwebs, a big oil drum. He could fit behind the drum and not be seen if he squatted with his butt close to the oil streaked floor. He would probably get his costume dirty but he had on the sweatshirt so it would only mess up the pants. He decided to risk it. He left the radio on the floor, snuck into the corner, brushed back some cobwebs, and squatted down.

The smell of oil was thick and it almost made him gag. He breathed mostly through his mouth and told himself it wasn't as bad as smelling puke, or Paul's beer breath. He heard the footsteps get closer and he was sure whoever was there was in the garage. Now that the sound was so near he was pretty sure it was only one person. Reggie poked his head around the oil drum to see who it was. He saw the glowing tip of a cigarette first and then his brother's long black hair. He stood up and came out of his hiding spot. Jesse was holding pillowcases stuffed with candy in each hand. He set them down and put his cigarette out on the concrete.

"All done trick or treating, little brother?" Jesse said.

"I didn't go," Reggie said.

Jesse nodded and swiped some of his long hair out of his face. He squinted at Reggie for a while then came up to him. Reggie thought he was going to ask him why he didn't go trick or treating.

"Let's go now," Jesse said. "Take off that sweatshirt and get a pillowcase,"

"Halloween's over."

"Not for you," he said. "Now come on."

Jesse dumped out the candy from one of his pillowcases and handed it to Reggie.

"I don't want to go anymore."

He felt his nose running like it always did before he cried. His face was hot and so was his body. The sweatshirt seemed too heavy now and it smelled like sweat and oil and he wanted to tear it off and run inside the house.

"I'm going to bed," Reggie said.

Jesse put his hand on Reggie's shoulder.

"Halloween's not over yet little brother," Jesse said. "So tell me what you want to do."

Reggie looked at the candy scattered on the floor, then across the street at Mr. Lecrone's. All the lights in the house had been turned off and the wind had blown out the candles inside the pumpkins. The only light came from a streetlight a couple houses down and from this Reggie could still make out the rounded orange shapes and their toothy smiles. Reggie put his radio away and wiped his nose on the sleeve of his sweatshirt.

"I know what I want to do," Reggie said.

Jesse smiled at him and set down his other pillowcases.

"Tell me little brother," he said. "Tell me."

LONG DIVISION

Autumn already. The maples on his street turning, sycamore bark scattered on sidewalks, a chill in the air when he woke up and took a short jog before work, it all gave Williams a sense that the summer hadn't really happened. Those warm, seemingly endless days of sitting with his neighbor, Caitlin, in the alley behind their houses, barbequing hamburgers and hotdogs, playing gin rummy or, if her children were there, go fish. Those hot afternoons where they'd walk together through their neighborhood, her kids racing out ahead of them, to the city pool. And best of all, the mornings when she'd invite him over for coffee and they'd sit quietly, watching steam rise from their mugs, and he'd feel an overwhelming sense of happiness, of belonging, which came partially from the smell of her freshly showered skin and the rich coffee and partially from just being so close to her. A woman he had secretly always loved but could never admit it to himself until just a short time ago. But as he looked around the room and saw the Kimball upright piano her husband had given her and the framed pictures of them together, the ones taken just before he died, Williams felt more like a visitor to a foreign country; he was welcome to enjoy the sights and the smells and the sounds but he couldn't stay and he would never really belong.

Now that it was fall he rarely saw her except for in brief moments. The other night he ran into her as they were wheeling out the dumpsters the night before garbage day. She wore only jeans and a t-shirt and he saw her shiver as she let go of the dumpster. The wind picked up, blowing a few orange leaves off the maples.

"It's getting cold out," he said.

She looked at him and folded her arms across her chest.

"Yeah," she said. "I guess it's jacket weather."

He nodded and they continued staring at each other. The wind died away and it was quiet except for the hum of the streetlight.

"Well," she said, uncrossing her arms. "I guess I'll go inside."

Another time he was standing in front of his bedroom mirror, buttoning his shirt and combing his hair before work, and he happened to look out his window to see her. Usually her second floor curtains were shut but she must have forgotten and he watched as she walked across her bedroom in a bathrobe she hadn't yet cinched at the waist. She was moving quickly through her room and with each hurried step he could see the brown and red checkered robe give way to quick flashes of her pale skin. For a moment he was so caught up watching her he forgot the distance separating them and the fact he couldn't go to her, slip off her robe, and feel the strong pulse at the base of her jaw.

Even though he sometimes went days without seeing her he could at least hear her every afternoon. As he sat in his study grading homework and tests he'd open his window and listen to her instructing her piano students, playing sections of Mozart and Chopin or maybe just scales. And he could always tell when it was Caitlin playing rather than the students. Sure, most of the students were beginners but even the more advanced kids, the ones who could play Mozart, didn't play every piece with the same tragic approach. In Caitlin's hands the most triumphant waltz sounded like a mockery of everything good about civilization, especially love and companionship. Sonatas, mazurkas, and nocturnes called to mind someone dying alone in a large and once great mansion.

At work — he taught math at the local high school — he couldn't concentrate. He would often find himself standing at the blackboard and forgetting which class, algebra or geometry, he was even teaching. There was one afternoon in particular where he really lost focus. He had been talking about triangles and then he suddenly broke off midsentence, staring out at the rows of faces looking back at him. Every time he tried to form a thought all he could think of was the photograph of Caitlin he had taken out of his wallet at lunchtime. It was a picture of her swimming at the city pool and it somehow captured her quiet and nervous energy. He had made a promise to himself to never look at it, especially not at work, but things sometimes happened.

The silence in the classroom seemed to grow and so did his sense of the awkward way he was standing; one arm raised partway, a worn piece of chalk clutched between his fingers. But still he couldn't move, or speak, or do anything except stare straight ahead. Eventually, someone in the front row coughed and Williams turned to face the blackboard where he saw an isosceles triangle he had drawn moments ago. He quickly scribbled the proof he had been talking about, took a deep breath, and resumed at least close to where he had left off. Over the next few minutes his mind cleared a little more but he had no conception of the reason behind what he was teaching. If one of the more sarcastic kids were to raise their hand and say, Why do we need to know this? he probably wouldn't have the answer. Because you need to pass Geometry to get your diploma. He might say that, if they really pressed him.

He hadn't seen her, really seen her, since Labor Day weekend. They were supposed to have gone on a trip together to her parents' cabin in northern Michigan. The cabin was built next to a lake and they went every year for the swimming, tubing, and fishing. This would be the first time in years she would go without her husband. Williams had been surprised at the invitation. They were drinking coffee one morning, her kids quietly playing in the next room, and she leaned over and touched his knee. He remembered staring at her hand, the chipped fingernails contrasting with the perfect shape and color of her fingers. It was her right hand, the hand without the ring, and he had wanted to attach some significance to the fact.

"Terry," she had said. "I have something to ask you. I guess you'd call it a favor."

He knew he'd say yes to whatever she asked of him. He still remembered what she said after she invited him: I don't want to be alone up there. At the time he didn't think to mention that she wouldn't really be alone; her two daughters would be there too. He started packing for the trip later that day even though they weren't going till next week. His bathing suit was faded and smelled of mothballs so he went out and bought a new one. He also bought sunscreen, beach towels, beach toys, and two plastic fishing rods for the girls. Probably Caitlin already had that kind of stuff — or at least they would find it at the cabin — but he wanted everything just in case. He knew it was ridiculous but he imagined a scene where he came to the rescue by having some much needed item. The two suitcases he had packed were still sitting by the front door, right where they were when he received her phone call saying she had changed her mind about him coming along.

By late October his state of mind hadn't changed much. If anything he felt worse; he couldn't even hear strains of music from next door now that the weather was usually cold enough for people to keep their windows closed. He bought records: Mozart, Chopin, Shumann. Her favorites, music he never would have thought twice about before. He played the records at night, after he finished grading tests and just before going to sleep. A few times he drank wine or beer as he listened but mostly he closed his eyes, imagined it was still summer, and thought about her, the smell of her skin. He remembered all of their conversations too. He remembered them even though she mainly talked about her husband. We married young, she had told him. But neither of us knew what marriage was. We could barely live in the same house together.

There was a night where, after playing records, he stood looking out his second story window at her house. No lights were on but the blinds weren't drawn and he thought he could see a person walk by the window. She did this several times and Williams kept staring. Eventually, Caitlin stopped in front of the window and it seemed like she was looking right at him. He knew he should step out of the way, close his curtain or somehow pretend he hadn't been watching her. But he felt detached from every part of his body except for his jaw, which was set tight, his teeth grinding against each other. Although he couldn't tell for sure it seemed like she was looking right at him too and he had almost worked up the nerve to smile or raise his hand when she shut the curtain. In the moment before her face disappeared, it looked like she was staring at the ground and shaking her head. He went to bed right afterwards but he couldn't get the image out of his mind and it stuck with him till the next morning when he woke from a bad night's sleep, went downstairs, and moved the suitcases to the basement utility room.

He called in to work a few times too, something he had never done before. He just needed a break. Overall he was doing better with not spacing out during class. However, there was one afternoon where he did a problem wrong on the board and a student, not even one of the smart kids from the front row, pointed it out. He had wanted to use a sick day so he wouldn't have to see his students the following afternoon but he made himself wait till later in the week.

On the days he called in he skipped his morning jog, stayed in bed late, and, after he finally got up, he sat in his office drinking coffee. From this spot he could see part of her living room: the piano, the couch, a couple paintings on the wall. Every now and then he saw her and always he would look away. Then he'd get up as if he had been planning on leaving the room. He would take his coffee and wander through his house, staring at the furniture, the walls, the clothes in his closet. Everything seemed so impersonal compared to what he saw in her house.

Sure, everything he owned was of good quality — he bought expensive furniture and carefully selected his clothes after studying the mannequins at upscale department stores — but none of it said anything about who he was. Williams remembered what his last girlfriend had said the first time she came over, Everything goes together so well. Her comment made him think of math: addition and subtraction, multiplication and division, numbers and shapes, problems he could solve without pen and paper. At first he had taken it as a compliment but then he saw how she was biting down on her lip and shaking her head.

He stayed the night at her place once. This was a couple days after she invited him up north. They had been watching a movie with her daughters and everyone but Williams fell asleep. He remembered watching the three of them and noting how they all kept one hand pressed against their neck, just below the jaw. After Caitlin woke up he rose from his seat, said he was leaving, and headed for the door.

"Wait," she said. "Let me put the girls to bed and then we'll say goodnight."

When she came back she took his hand and led him to the couch. They sat down, still holding hands, both of them looking at the blank T.V. screen. Before long she turned to him and said, "It's too quiet, don't you think?"

He shrugged. He wanted to hear her play something on the piano but knew it would be too loud with the girls being asleep.

"I think it's too quiet," she said.

She grabbed the remote, turned the television on to a channel that played music videos, and laid on top of him.

She did all this without letting go of his hand. They made out for what seemed like hours and when he closed his eyes Williams could almost imagine himself fifteen years younger, exploring the taste and feel of a girl's body for the first time in his parent's basement. At some point they took off their shirts. They lay sideways with their bodies pressed against each other, not kissing, but just enjoying the feel of warm skin. They stayed like this for what seemed like a long time and then she sat up and let out a loud breath.

"What do you want?" she said.

It seemed like the whole summer had been leading up to this moment and he answered her right away.

"Everything."

He ran his hand along her hip and then moved it to the inside of her thigh.

"That's not what I was talking about."

He nodded, took his hand off her leg, and touched her cheek.

Afterwards there was a feeling in the air like they had gotten away with something. Neither of them looked at each other although they held hands for a while. He didn't look at her until he thought she was falling asleep; her hand fell away from his and her breathing turned shallow. The T.V. was still on and he stared at it for a while, trying to decide whether to wake her or not. He couldn't imagine them both sleeping there the whole night; the girls waking up to see their mom and the next door neighbor half-naked on the living room couch. Every time he reached to touch her shoulder his hand seemed to stop on its own. Then he'd look at the blue light of the television on her face, her hair, the slope of her shoulders and he'd tell himself he'd wait a few more minutes before waking her. Eventually though, even he fell asleep.

When he woke up she was standing above him. She was fully dressed and he couldn't remember her getting up or putting her shirt on. The T.V. was off.

"I guess I should go," he said.

She bent down, grabbed his shirt from the floor, and handed it over.

"You don't have to," she said. "You could stay here."

He pulled on his shirt.

"On the couch?"

She nodded and looked away from him.

"It's the best I can do right now."

She walked out of the room before he could say anything. After she left he tried to be O.K. with the situation; he lay back down, shut his eyes, and tried to sleep but he kept imagining how the girls would react when they saw him in the morning. Eventually he gathered up his shoes and left, hoping she was asleep and didn't hear him slip out.

Her husband died in a car accident last winter. For weeks Caitlin's driveway was filled with cars, relatives from both sides coming to stay with her and help out with the girls. Neighbors stopped by almost every day, bringing with them casserole dishes, pies, trays of baked goods, so much that he wondered how one family, even one with a lot of houseguests, could possibly finish it all. He waited a month before going over there. It was a weeknight, around eight-thirty, and he figured her girls would probably be asleep. He walked out of his house, up his front walk, down the sidewalk a short way, and then up her front walk. It would have been quicker to cut across his yard and then hers but it seemed wrong somehow; it had snowed the night before and his bootprints would have broken the yard of untouched snow.

She answered her door right away, like she wasn't at all surprised to have another visitor. He said he was sorry he hadn't stopped by sooner.

"That's fine," she said. "It's been crazy over here."

She motioned him inside, crossed the room, and sat down on the piano bench. She sat on it sideways so that she wasn't facing him or the piano. The only seat close by was a large sofa with cushions that sank under his weight. She didn't seem to notice. He told her he was sorry about her husband. She nodded, dragging her fingers across the piano keys, stopping every now and then as if she had just remembered a song she wanted to play.

"If you ever need someone to watch the girls I'm home in the afternoons."

She nodded again and turned so she was directly facing him.

"Charlie used to sleep on that couch," she said. "When he was home, anyway."

Williams knew her husband had been a truck driver although he had never given much thought to how much he was gone.

"It's strange," she said. "The girls never asked me why he slept out here. They probably thought it was normal."

She laughed and quickly turned away from him, bringing her hand up to her mouth as she moved, as if to cover her laughter.

"I should get home," he said. "If you ever need me to watch the kids though."

She ran her fingers across the piano keys once more then stood up.

"I feel like I should miss him more," she said. "He was my husband."

She looked at him and raised her eyes in a way that suggested she wanted a response.

"Well," he said.

Her eyes got wider and he opened his mouth to say more but nothing came out.

One afternoon he looked out his window to see Caitlin's girls raking his front yard. They already had a pile that was almost as tall as they were. He watched them for a while and before long they had set down their rakes and were jumping into the pile, tossing fistfuls of red and yellow maple leaves into the air. He went outside to the garage, grabbed his rake, and joined them out front. Both girls stopped jumping around when they saw him. Their cheeks were flushed from the cold and he could see their breath whenever they exhaled. They waved him over.

"Terry," they both said as he came closer.

"That's quite a pile you got there," he said.

Ellen, the younger girl, looked up at him and smiled.

"We're helping," she said.

"Yeah," Louisa said. "I need some help with my homework and mom said we should do something for you."

Williams nodded and said that was nice of them. Ellen smiled again and jumped back into the leaves.

"What kind of homework is it?" he said.

Louisa frowned and then said, "Long division."

He looked across his yard over to their house. He thought he saw Caitlin standing by one of the front windows.

"That's hard," he told her.

He helped Louisa with her homework every day for a week. She came over after school let out. Before they got to the homework she'd take out a bag of cookies, usually oatmeal raisin, her favorite, and split them with Williams. She always turned down the glass of milk he offered. They hardly spoke. He wanted to tell her how he missed spending time with her and Ellen, watching them practice their dives at the city pool, playing Go Fish, and barbequing their hot dogs the way they liked, charred all around. But since she never brought up anything about the summer he kept his mouth shut. He was surprised at how quiet she was though. Normally Louisa always had something to say but that was when her mom and sister were around. Aside from her saying hello or asking if she did a problem right, the only sound was her writing. It reminded him of how all the times he was alone with Caitlin they never said much.

One day though, Louisa stopped in the middle of a problem, looked up at him and said, "Maybe tomorrow you should come over to my house."

He smiled and nodded.

"Yeah," she said. "Your kitchen's freezing. My fingers get cold."

"Oh," he said. "I have a space heater I could bring up from the basement. Would that be all right?"

She said that would be fine. He wanted to tell her that he couldn't do this anymore but they still hadn't talked about remainders.

The next day he saw Caitlin in his yard. She was raking his leaves — the girls had only finished half the job and he didn't care enough to say anything. Williams threw on his coat, stepped outside, and walked over to her. She said hello and smiled. Up close she looked different than he remembered; she had on glasses instead of contacts and her hair seemed more red than brown. He didn't care for either change; she had the look of a woman who had moved on from something.

"I like your hair," he said. "The glasses too."

She nodded.

"The girls don't like it. They say it makes me look like this teacher at their school."

He pointed at the pile of leaves she had going.

"You don't have to do this," he said. "I was just going to leave them there for the winter. Someone told me it's good for the grass."

She stopped raking and took off her glasses. She held them up to her face like she was checking them for smudges.

"Louisa tells me you're really helping her out. I appreciate you doing that."

"She's really doing most of the work."

She took one hand off the rake and touched his arm. He noticed she wasn't wearing gloves and he was surprised at how dry her hands were. Probably they would blister from raking if she wasn't careful. He was about to offer her a pair of his gloves when she said his name.

"Terry," she said. "I think we should talk."

They finished the leaves together and then went to her place. He waited on the sofa while she made coffee. It was dusk outside, the sky a dark purple like before a big rain. A few boys were in the street, practicing moves on their skateboards. Every now and then one of them would look his way and smile. The boys seemed to like having an audience because every time they did a new trick they'd catch his eye as if to say, Did you see that one? In a few years he would probably have those boys in his freshman algebra class although by then they wouldn't seek his approval or even like him very much.

Williams watched them for a couple more minutes until Caitlin came into the room. She handed him his coffee and then shut the curtains. He could still hear the boys: the clack of wheels against pavement after a jump and the shouting that followed. Caitlin took a seat close by him on the sofa. She blew on her coffee a few times before taking a sip.

"I think we both moved too fast," she said. "And I probably talked about Charlie too much."

He started to shake his head but she cut him off.

"I should have been talking about you more. You're so good with Ellen and Louisa. Jesus, Charlie couldn't even remember their birthdays."

She laughed and then took a sip of her coffee. Outside, one of the boys was shouting and then the sound of the skateboards trailed off like they were riding away.

"I'm sure he wasn't as bad as you make it seem," he said. "There must have been something between you."

She set her coffee mug down on the end table, crossed her legs, and looked around the room. Williams couldn't be sure but it seemed like she was staring at each of the photographs. When she was finished she uncrossed her legs and said, "Did you even talk to him?"

He told her they had only spoken a couple times. What he did remember was seeing Charlie playing catch with Ellen and Louisa in their front yard. Williams mentioned this to Caitlin too.

"They looked like they were having a lot of fun."

"You're not listening to me, Terry," she said. "I'm trying to say that I think you're a decent man."

She put a hand on his knee. He had been holding his coffee mug with two hands but now he took one away and set it on hers.

"So what does that mean?" he said.

Apparently it meant their relationship would be like it was before. They saw each other all the time except now that it was winter they did puzzles, watched television, and took the girls sledding. The red faded from her hair, she rarely wore her glasses, and she used a self tanner so altogether she looked like she did over the summer. She still talked about Charlie a lot, pretty much whenever the girls weren't in the room. She always apologized but Williams said he didn't mind. He figured it was her way of moving on. Usually her comments about him weren't of much substance but one evening she surprised him by talking about their sex life. The girls were staying over at their grandma's house and they had cooked dinner together. Afterwards Caitlin had made a fire while he washed dishes. When he was done he joined her by the fireplace. It was almost Christmas and the mantle was hung with stockings and the photographs had been cleared away to make room for various decorations.

They each said that dinner was good and then they were quiet for a while until Williams asked if she would play him something on the piano. He asked her, expecting to hear her usual response which was, "No, it always seems like work to me now." But if she heard him, she didn't show it. Instead, she told him that the one thing she didn't hate about the marriage was the sex.

"We hardly spoke to each other," she said. "But we still made love. And to keep it interesting we'd play games, pretend we were strangers. I'd lie in bed with the lights off and I knew he'd get up from the couch and come to me but I didn't know when. It got to be so that was the only way either of us liked it."

As she spoke he stared at the flames until his eyes lost focus. He tried not to hear the nostalgic quality of her voice. When she came to the end she laughed and then said, "See, Terry. You really don't want to be with me."

He had the feeling that she was somehow testing him and that if he spoke too soon or waited too long she'd quit seeing him again. He kept looking at the fire, as if the random flickering held an answer. When the silence had gone on for longer than he could take, he turned to her, smiled what felt like a weak smile, and said her name; it was all he could think to say.

"Maybe it would help if you told me about the women you've been with."

He shook his head and turned back to the fire.

"There isn't that much to tell."

She slept with him that night and he felt like it was mainly out of pity. They were tender, almost careful with each other and they both seemed to fear the awkwardness that would come when it was over. And so they spent a lot of time kissing and asking each other what felt the best, as if this could solve their problem. Afterwards, when there was nothing left to ask, they laid by the fire some more, holding each other and looking at the flames and the Christmas decorations. When the logs got down to a few embers she asked if he wanted to stay. He looked around the room, first over to the Christmas tree and the presents he had bought for the girls, then over to the couch.

"It won't always be like this," she said. "I'm trying to change."

She leaned over, kissed him, and then rose to her feet. He thought about saying that he was trying to change too and decided it would sound weak.

"I'll get you some blankets," she said. "Maybe that's why you left early last time."

She said this in a tone that somehow didn't place blame on either of them. Still, he got up and said he was leaving. His voice was quiet though and he wasn't looking at her.

"What if I played you something?" she said. "Would you stay then?"

He paused for a moment as if he was really weighing this choice. Then he nodded and made his way to the couch.

He woke up to the sound of his name and at first he thought he had been dreaming. But he heard it again, Terry, it said, and he knew it was Caitlin although he couldn't tell if she was asleep or awake; her voice had a hollow, far-off quality he hadn't heard before. He got up from the sunken cushions with some difficulty and crossed the room, walking slow and waiting for the reassurance of her voice calling out again. When he got to the Christmas tree he paused to look at the brightly lit branches, the decorations, and the presents underneath.

She said his name again, louder and clearer than before, and he hurried through the hallway to her room. But when he reached the open doorway he stopped, although she was telling him to come in, "I changed my mind."

And he knew he would do as she said; but for several minutes he stood in the doorway, staring into the darkness, waiting for his eyes to focus, as if he could see not just her dim figure in the bed but also the man he was becoming.

ON THE BEACH

The boy waited till late in the day, his mother asleep in her beach chair, to ask if he could go swimming.

"It's getting late, son," his father said. "We'll be leaving soon."

"I want to go in the water," the boy said.

The father pointed to a sign which showed a figure swimming crossed out in bold red. No words accompanied it. The boy shook his head.

"I don't understand. The water looks fine."

For several moments the father stared at the water, now and then squinting when the sun was too bright. He agreed with his son. The water did look O.K. In fact, it appeared to be the same color as when he used to swim here as a boy. But the sign, as well as all the news reports, said it wasn't safe.

"There's something wrong," he said. "Maybe farther out in the water where we can't see it."

The boy looked out at the water and bit his lip.

"What about somewhere else," he said. "Maybe if we go further up the beach there won't be signs."

His father thought about explaining that the water would be the same no matter where they went but knew this logic would mean nothing to his son. At some point that summer he had promised his son that they would go swimming, and he knew the boy would find some way to hold the broken promise over him in the form of hurt looks.

"We can try another spot," the father said. "But if there are signs there then we'll have to go swimming another time."

The boy smiled and skipped a stone on the water.

"Should we see if mom wants to come?"

The father looked over at his wife. Her breathing seemed shallower than normal and the slight wrinkles near her eyes looked more noticeable than before. And the longer he stared at her, the older she appeared. His son seemed to feel this way too, only he didn't say so out loud; it was obvious from the way he squinted and then rubbed his eyes.

"We should let her sleep," the father said.

Even before he finished speaking the boy was nodding.

They had walked about a mile up the beach and still hadn't found any place to swim. Every hundred yards or so a sign was posted telling them not to go in the water. Each sign looked older than the last: the paint peeling in some spots and the color fading to grays and browns. After a while, the father even started doubting his memory of swimming here as a boy. His son didn't seem discouraged, though. He ignored the signs and kept walking, stopping only to skip a stone or inspect pieces of washed up sea life.

Every so often they'd encounter someone, and the boy would say hello and ask why they couldn't swim. The first person, a young man with traces of sunscreen blotched across his face, said it was because of the undertow.

"It'll suck you right under," he said. "It'll drag your head across the bottom where all the shells will cut you up."

The father knew this wasn't true at all. This beach had been popular in part because there was no undertow, but he didn't say this to his son. The boy raised his eyebrows at this explanation but kept walking.

The next person they came across was an old man dressed in a white linen suit and a straw hat. He was reading a book with a very long and confusing title. When the boy asked why they couldn't swim, he pointed out at the water.

"It's the power plant," he said. "It's been polluting the water for years."

The man slammed the book shut as if to emphasize his point. This explanation, the father knew, was only partially right. There was a power plant located on a small island, but it featured a new process that gave off no harmful byproducts. The energy company had assured the public of this years ago. He tried arguing with the old man, explaining to him how there had been no alternative to the new plant, but the old man kept cutting him off. After only a few minutes of this, the father grew tired. He sighed and turned to his son.

"We should get back now. Your mother is probably wondering where we went."

The boy kept on, as if he hadn't heard his father at all. His dad started to yell for him to stop, but even he started to wonder if there was any truth to his words. He had the sudden feeling that maybe she wouldn't be there waiting for them. While he was having this thought, the boy ran further up the beach, leaving him no choice but to catch up.

As they walked, the two noticed that the texture of the sand changed. Before it had been fine, soft, almost powdery, but now it was coarse and scattered with rocks. There were no people on the beach or boats out in the water. The signs had stopped appearing at regular intervals. By sunset they had gone past where the father had explored when he was a kid.

"Can we swim now?" the boy said.

The father looked back in the direction they had come and then up ahead. There were no signs in sight.

"Let's go a little further," he said.

It was sunset now, and the pinkish-orange sky above the water looked like an advertisement for a resort. The boy and his dad kept walking until they came upon a woman wearing no clothes. She was standing right at the shoreline, letting the waves wash over her feet. In many ways she looked like his wife except her body was dark like she had been out in the sun too long. He wondered if his son saw the resemblance, too.

"You're naked," the boy said. "How come?"

The woman turned to face them but said nothing. The boy walked up closer to her and asked if they could swim now. For a long while she just stared, her face unmoving, eyes near shut like how an animal sleeps but still keeps watch for predators. Eventually her head tilted down in what might have been a nod. The boy looked to his dad for confirmation.

"Sure," he said. "Let's go in the water."

In truth, he wasn't sure if the woman had given them permission, but he didn't care anymore. They had walked a long way, and he wanted to cool off. So they left the woman standing on the shore and raced into the water. They hadn't gone very far before the boy asked why the water was so warm.

"We have to go further out I guess."

The boy nodded but he seemed unsure. He looked back to the woman on the shore as if she would give them a better answer. The woman was still there, but she wasn't looking at them.

She appeared to be pointing at the horizon where the sun had just gone down. In the deeper water further out the surface turned pinkish-red. The boy opened his mouth but his dad cut him off.

"It's just plankton," he said. "I remember reading it can do that sometimes. Something about depletion or decomposition."

"Should we go back?" the boy said.

"We've come too far," his dad said. "We at least need to cool off."

The boy nodded, but he wasn't looking at his dad. They continued on. The water grew colder right at the point when the boy could no longer stand with his head above water. The shock of the sudden change was like nothing either of them could remember experiencing. They started swimming, going out into deeper water until the cold became too much and then they returned to shallower, warmer water. The sensation they felt was beyond pleasure or pain.

They lost track of time, and when they thought to look around it was completely dark except for a fire on the shore. The woman sat hunched over the blaze, rocking and nodding in a slow rhythm. She was moving her mouth now, too, but even when the father and son swam within earshot, they could tell the simple and archaic language she spoke was beyond their understanding.

John Abbott

I THINK YOU SHOULD LEAVE NOW

His house was the only one on the block still lit. Besides the streetlights and the occasional porch light there was nothing, not even a hint that any of his neighbors were awake. He had expected to see the blue glow of a television set or perhaps an upstairs window curtain, backlit from a lamp kept on by a child too afraid to fall asleep for fear of what they might dream. But it was as though the whole neighborhood had gone to bed, leaving him to do as he pleased. He could have walked, unnoticed, through backyards and alleyways, snatching up anything people had been too careless to put away.

Not long ago he probably would've grabbed a few things, but right now this opportunity didn't interest him at all. He was too caught up with what he was doing now, standing at the end of his curving front walkway and looking at his house, counting how many windows he could see and how many lights he had left on. This is how my house looks at night, he thought. For some time he stood there, arms folded tight against his chest, his longish hair sweeping across his vision whenever the breeze picked up. It was cool out, especially for May, and to Reece it had the feel of early autumn. Only the faint scent of lilac in the air confirmed that it was spring.

Before too long Reece found himself yawning and he knew it was time he got to bed. He had been up since five a.m., packing his few belongings and then moving them here, to his new house that no one, including himself, thought he could ever afford. His arms were sore and his mind could only complete the most basic thoughts and yet he wasn't ready for the lights to go out. Although it didn't make sense he felt that the house would disappear or cease to exist and he would wake up in the foul smelling apartment he had shared with a variety of transients, junkies, and thieves. Also, he knew it would be hard to fall

54

asleep in a new environment and the thought of lying awake the rest of the night scared him a little.

So he walked through the tall, dewy grass — he would need to mow it soon, once he bought a lawnmower — and around to the back of his house. The smell of lilac was stronger now although he didn't remember seeing any bushes when he was outside earlier, checking out the condition of the yard, exploring the boundaries of what was his. Short, thorny bushes which he didn't know the name of lined the edge of the house and he made sure to avoid these on his way. When he reached the backyard he came within sight of the small, one car garage and a light positioned above the door lit up in the same moment he noticed it was there, as if the light existed purely because of his will. My garage has a motion light, he thought. He stared at this discovery for some time, letting it sink in, wondering how he hadn't noticed it before. At some point he turned his head toward the rest of the backyard. Toward the farthest edge, where a chain link fence separated his yard from a neighbor's, he saw something which he didn't quite believe at first: a woman sitting by herself on a low bench made of black wrought iron. He hadn't noticed either one of these sights earlier. The possibility that this woman could have brought the bench with her and placed it under the sycamore tree seemed almost more unbelievable than the fact a woman was in his yard.

Before he could really try and make sense of it all, she called out to him.

"Hey babe," she said, her voice hoarse and strained like she had been running. "It took me a while to find you."

He walked through the tall grass, the moisture soaking the cuffs of his jeans, until he reached where she was sitting. She sat with her legs folded under her butt and her hands gripping the arms of the bench like she might fall off otherwise. The motion light had switched off but the lights from his house were enough for Reece to see the track marks on her pale, skinny arms.

"You didn't say you were going to leave the lights on for me," she said. "That would have made this a lot easier."

He folded his arms, shook his head, and asked her what she was talking about.

"I don't know who you are," he said.

She unfolded her legs and let go of her grip on the bench. After laughing for a moment she stood up and walked close to him. They were now less than an arms length apart. She smelled strongly of clove cigarettes but even these couldn't mask the unmistakable smell of someone who hadn't washed in days. He remembered this from his days at the apartment when it was a rare thing to have running water, rarer still to have water that didn't feel like ice against your skin.

"Is that how you want to do this?" she said. "Pretend we're strangers so that everything feels new again?"

Her breath as she spoke caused him to take a step back. It was a sweet, putrid smell like decaying flowers.

"I said I didn't know you."

Reece pointed in the direction he thought she had come from and told her she should leave. She laughed again, a high, piercing one note blast that Reece feared would wake somebody. When she was through she told him that she had nowhere she could go.

"Don't you remember what that's like?" she said.

He looked all around to see if any lights came on nearby, but all the houses, except his own, were still dark. Overhead the sky seemed a shade lighter, suggesting morning might be closer than Reece had thought.

"We met when you were homeless," she said. "We were both standing in line at the mission. I remember when we first saw each other there was this look we shared that shamed us both. We were too good for that place and yet there we were. When we looked at each other it was like we both swore we'd never stand in one of those lines again."

He took another step away from her and looked at the bench. It was still there. It looked very solid.

"I don't remember that," he said.

She closed the distance between them and touched his arm. Her fingertips felt cold and dry.

"Well, I guess you were kind of strung out then," she said. "I suppose I was too."

He backed up faster, taking long strides that took him within range of the motion light again. The sudden beam against his face made him feel like a burglar caught by someone in the house. He desperately wished he could turn it off.

"But you've done well for yourself," she said, still following him, matching him step for step. "You look good, not as skinny as before. You're eyes still look hungry, though. It's hard to change that."

He took a few more steps so that the light didn't catch him directly and, after his eyes readjusted, an idea came to him.

"What's my name?" he said. "If we were really together you'd know my name."

She laughed and shook her head.

"Names never mattered with us," she said. "We were in love. It was the two of us against the world; but then you left me."

He turned his back to her and kept walking.

"I'm going inside," he said. "Don't follow me anymore."

He was running now, the thorny bushes clawing at his jeans as he ran alongside the house. The smell of lilac had disappeared and all that was left was her. He ran faster, his lungs swelling and leaping with his every step. Before long he had gained the front porch by jumping up the three steps in one bound. Without looking back he shut the door, locked it, and leaned against the wall to recover his breath. He wanted to turn off all the lights but he wasn't sure if he was ready for the feelings that would bring.

"I'm still here," she said.

It sounded like she was on the porch although he hadn't heard her walk up the steps. If the front window wasn't left open partway — he did this to air out the musty smell in the house — he might not have heard her. He flipped one of the three switches without knowing what it controlled. The light above his head went out. My foyer is dark now.

"I just need a place to crash," she said. "I'm coming down pretty hard."

He flipped another switch and a light in the next room shut off. The dining room is dark too. He told her that he was going to bed now.

"You fucker," she said, her voice strangely quiet. "Don't leave me alone like this. I'd never do this to you."

He hit the last switch and the porch went dark. He heard a flickering noise from outside and saw the streetlights go out. The sky outside his front windows was purple-black, turning gray toward what must have been the east. It seemed impossible that morning had almost arrived. Had he really been wandering around his house and yard for that long?

"Do you remember the first night we slept together?" she said.

Her voice was still quiet although now it had taken on a reflexive quality that reminded Reece of how children talk to themselves as they play, whether or not anyone is listening.

"Afterwards I told you about this dream I always have on the nights when I'm clean. In the dream I suddenly realize I don't have to live the way I've been living. I can change and I don't have to hurt anyone ever again."

He heard the porch boards creak like maybe she was lying down. Soon enough someone would be coming to deliver the paper and they'd see a junkie sprawled out on his porch.

"The feeling wasn't like anything else I'd experienced. It was better than shooting up. It was kind of religious I guess, but without someone preaching at you. And for a couple hours after waking up I'd walk around feeling like a damn saint or something, smiling at everything and everyone like I knew something they didn't."

Without meaning to he yawned, a really big one that she probably heard. He expected this to piss her off so he started walking up the stairs.

"Wait," she said. "I haven't gotten to the good part yet."

Her voice sounded closer, like she was inside rather than on the porch. The ripe smell of her body seemed close too but he didn't want to turn around to see if she was there. He couldn't seem to keep climbing the stairs either, despite the fact that the second floor, lit up like it was, seemed very welcoming.

"Do you remember what you said about my dream?"

When he didn't respond she repeated her question again and again, pleading with him to say something. Finally, when her voice got to where it made his throat get tight he spoke up.

"No," he said. "Because I don't even know you."

"You smiled at me and said, "You have that one too." And then I laughed and held you and I knew we had something good. Something real."

His chest felt tight now and he was suddenly very warm. He wanted to yank off the long sleeved plaid shirt and let the cool air wash over him.

"I wouldn't have said that. That doesn't sound like me at all. I would have said that it was just a dream."

59

Before she could say anything else Reece hurried up the rest of the stairs, fumbling with the buttons on his shirt as he went. He turned off the lights in the hallway and in the bathroom, finished taking off his shirt, and walked into his room. And as he hesitated with his finger on the light switch, the one that would make his house completely dark, he hoped that what he had just said was true.

DUPLEXITY

Duke would not stop barking at the woods. Penny tried to ignore him, but she knew from experience it would only get worse: the barking would turn to crying and then a whimper that just about killed her. She turned to her husband and said, "He misses the country, Greer. I should take him for a walk in the woods."

Greer looked up from his comps — he worked as a realtor — and said he would prefer it if Duke just shut up. "He's going to get us evicted," he added. Before she could remind him that the other half of the duplex was empty he told her the woods weren't safe. "It's where the junkies and winos hang out." If Greer realized he had said roughly the same thing to her on at least two other occasions, he did nothing to show it.

"I guess I'll go get him," Penny said.

Greer nodded, gathered together his papers, and stuffed them in his briefcase. He then stood from the table and told her he was going to show a loft downtown. As he was halfway out the door, he turned back to her and said, "I know what you're thinking, Penny, but I can't have you going into those woods."

His words had the feel of an afterthought, something Greer felt he should say rather than something he really meant. Penny gave some vague, yet affirmative, response and then Greer was gone. She waited a couple minutes and then filled a travel mug with coffee, put on a jacket, and grabbed Duke's leash. Outside it had just rained and there was the smell of wet leaves and earth in the air. She knew Duke would love it out in the woods. Back at their old home in the country, they didn't even need to chain Duke up. Their nearest neighbor lived close to a mile away and Duke was good about staying away from the road. But here in the city there were leash laws, more neighbors, and busier streets.

As she got close to the woods, Penny expected Duke to start barking, but he just kept sniffing the ground. There was a woodchip trail that she followed at first. Since she didn't know how large the woods were yet, she figured it would be a smart idea because she would be able to find her way back easily. As she walked, Penny sipped at her coffee and took note of the sycamore and black oak trees, but mostly she just watched Duke.

Before she had gone far she saw a little clearing where an old brown blanket lay wadded up beside several empty beer bottles. Without really meaning to, she said out loud, "I guess you were right, Greer." Lately she had gotten into the habit of talking to herself this way, mostly as she unpacked the boxes that cluttered their new place.

Duke sniffed the blanket, one of the bottles, and then moved on. Penny considered turning around but decided against it, mainly because she was sick of unpacking. If she did come across someone, there was a good chance it would be someone harmless, an old wino perhaps. And if it was someone dangerous, well, she had Duke with her, and he was about the best protection she could ask for: she had watched helplessly from her back porch once as he killed a deer in less than a minute.

A while later she came across a man walking the trail. He was tall with curly gray-black hair pouring out of a faded yellow baseball cap. He also had a long, untrimmed beard that reminded her of a serial killer she had once seen on the news. She wondered if the blanket and bottles she had seen belonged to him. Duke ran to him, yanking her along in the process.

"How long have you had this dog?" he said.

Duke started barking, and she told him to be quiet.

"Five years," she said. "I've had him five years. Why?"

The man took a step forward and immediately Duke tried to sniff him and lick his hands.

"I had a dog that looked just like this and he took off five years ago."

He reached down to pet Duke, but Penny yanked on the leash hard enough to pull Duke away.

"How long did you say you've had him?"

The man dragged out the last word into two syllables, highlighting what Penny now realized was a mistake on her part: She shouldn't have said that Duke was a boy.

"Look," she said. "I've had him since he was a puppy. I need to get going now."

The man reached out for Duke again, but this time she wasn't quick enough to pull Duke back before he could lick the man's fingers. Without really thinking, she yanked the leash so hard Duke yelped once and turned to look at her. Then she pulled her dog closer and started walking. Over the crunch of leaves and woodchips she could still hear the man talking, asking her how long she's had him and where she got him from. Between the noise from her footsteps and the rapid thrum of her pulse she couldn't tell if he was following her or not. It wasn't until a few minutes later, once she couldn't hear his voice, that she realized she had gone further into the woods instead of back toward home.

Greer came home late that night. He smelled strongly of beer and the cigars his friend smoked. Penny knew from experience this meant he hadn't made any sales. Whenever Greer had a bad day he and his friend would meet at the cigar club for an hour or so after work, drinking and smoking and reminiscing about the days before the real estate market tanked. He greeted her and asked if she wanted to order a pizza. She said that sounded fine.

"Same kind as last night?" he said, bending down to scratch Duke underneath his chin.

Duke lifted his head up and opened his mouth as if smiling in appreciation.

"Someone wants to steal Duke, Greer."

Greer stopped scratching the dog and looked at her. She proceeded to tell him what happened out in the woods, leaving out a few details like how she'd gone the wrong way after seeing the man, which led to her getting lost for awhile, not in the woods themselves but in the unfamiliar part of the neighborhood the trail spit her out in. Also, she had been so shaken by the time she got home that she had accidentally unlocked the wrong door of their duplex; she had keys to both units because the landlord had given them a discount on the rent in exchange for Greer showing it to potential renters. Stepping inside the other place always threw her for a moment, both because the layout was completely reversed and because its emptiness offered up such possibility for change it was both terrifying and exhilarating.

"Did he try to hurt you or Duke?" Greer said once she finished the story.

"No," she said. "He thinks we have his dog, though."

Greer stood up and walked over to the phone.

"He's probably just some homeless guy who had too much to drink today."

Up until this moment, Penny probably would've agreed, but looking back she realized the man hadn't smelled like booze at all. In fact, he didn't even smell like he needed a shower, whereas Greer, with the sour mixture of cheap cigars, beer, and disappointment soaked into his clothes, smelled like someone who did. She was about to bring up this point, but Greer had already dialed the phone number and was placing their order. As she listened to him on the phone it occurred to Penny that Greer hadn't even brought up how she shouldn't have gone into the woods in the first place. She tried not to think about whether this meant he was being kind or that he didn't care.

The next day Penny only let Duke outside for short periods of time, and she made sure she kept a close watch on him. When it came time for Duke's walk she decided to just stay in the neighborhood. Since moving, she hadn't ventured out of the apartment much. The neighborhood didn't seem dangerous, but it didn't seem inviting either. The couple times she had taken Duke out, the only people she had seen stared at her from their front porches, making her feel like an outsider. Penny sensed they could feel her embarrassment at the condition that most of the houses were in: the crumbling cinder blocks holding up porches, paint peeling or siding falling off, unkempt lawns strewn with children's toys or cigarette butts.

Even though she didn't have to deal with these feelings too often, she still couldn't understand Greer's decision to move here since the location wasn't that great, and he was always going on about how much that mattered when you looked for a place to live. Out of the three places they had looked at, the one they chose was in the worst location — and she liked it the least. The only conclusion she could come up with was that he had pushed them into it to punish her because she hadn't asked her parents for a loan like he had wanted her to. His theory was that they just needed to squeak by for a few more months, maybe half a year, until the market picked up. She had thought it was a bad idea, one that would only put them in debt, so she had refused; her refusal had led to several fights, which only made the time surrounding their move worse.

She tried to distract herself from these memories by walking faster. Duke responded and broke out into a run. She sped up so he wasn't dragging her, and before long she was running faster than she had in a while. The rhythmic pounding of her feet against the sidewalk felt good, gave her something to focus on. Duke was enjoying himself, too. They kept up their pace for a couple blocks until she saw a turquoise van blocking a driveway. She slowed down to watch for traffic, stepped out into the street, and walked around the van.

Before she could go much further, she heard someone calling after. At first the words weren't clear, but the man kept repeating himself: "Where'd you say you got that dog?"

She turned and saw the bearded man from the other day. The driver's side door to the van was open like he had just gotten out because of her. She told Duke to hurry up, but he ignored her and sat there wagging his tail.

"Damnit, Duke! I told you to c'mon," she said.

She could feel the blood rushing to her face as she spoke. She didn't know if she was angrier at the man for harassing her or at Duke for not listening.

"My dog looked just like this," he said, walking closer and stopping to bend down so he was at eye level with the dog.

For a moment he simply crouched there looking at Duke, and during this time she got a better look at him than she did the other day. He was younger than she had realized, for one thing. Probably he was only forty instead of being in his late fifties or early sixties. The amount of gray in his beard had thrown her off, but now she could see his face didn't have too many wrinkles. His eyes were a soft brown that looked watery at this particular moment. She pulled Duke closer but felt some of the tension leave her body.

"I'm sorry you lost your dog," she said. "But I've had him since he was a puppy. So I know he's not yours."

She realized she was speaking too slowly, the way some people spoke to foreigners, little kids, or the elderly.

"What did you say his name was?"

"I'm sorry you lost your dog," she said. "But I need to be going."

As she walked away, she concentrated hard on going the right direction toward home.

She didn't hear the door open. She only looked away from her magazine when Duke got up. Before she could say or do anything she heard Greer's voice.

"Penny? Are you in here?"

She looked around at the empty kitchen and then walked toward the door. Duke was wagging his tail and licking Greer's hands. Without stopping to pet the dog, Greer came over to her and hugged her tight.

"You and Duke weren't there when I got home," he said. "I was getting worried."

"I'm sorry," she said. "I came over here to get away from all the boxes and lost track of time."

He held her for another moment and she breathed in the smell of his body. The mix of his cologne, pencil shavings, and his natural smell reminded her of their previous home; she was grateful he hadn't gone drinking after work.

"I saw that man again," she said. "I don't think he's homeless."

He stepped away from her and petted Duke, who was still wagging his tail. She explained how the man still thought Duke was his and how he owned a vehicle.

"He might even live around here," she said.

"I still think he's probably harmless," Greer said as he walked toward the door. "But at least he doesn't know where we live."

They ordered pizza again, making it three nights in a row. Penny had suggested going out to dinner, but Greer said he needed to update some listings online.

"Maybe another night this week," he said.

Penny nodded. She remembered a remark one of her old coworkers had made once. Something about how three of something made a chain. The remark was in reference to the coffee shop where they worked opening up a new location. She knew that she was taking the idea completely out of context, but she couldn't get past the imagery of a chain, the heavy iron and permanence.

"I thought one of the reasons we chose this apartment was so we'd be closer to downtown," she said.

Greer looked up from his computer quickly, as if he had been slapped. She guessed that it was because she had used the word apartment. She knew Greer felt ashamed about renting instead of owning because he worked as a realtor; he felt it was akin to an overweight person teaching an aerobics class.

"You're right," he said. "Maybe we can go out for dinner and a show sometime soon."

"When?"

Greer looked back at his computer, typed for a second, then looked around. She couldn't tell for sure, but it looked like he was counting the number of boxes he could see. Even though she had unpacked quite a few boxes already, the room still seemed claustrophobic. It didn't help that Greer hadn't agreed to sell some of their stuff or put it into storage when they moved.

"Maybe after we're settled in more," he said.

She pushed aside her untouched plate of pizza and stood up. "Maybe that would happen faster if you helped out more."

She couldn't sleep that night. It was a combination of things: the man who wanted Duke, the argument with Greer, the unfamiliar noises of their apartment, and the fear of having another nightmare about wandering through a neighborhood where it was continuously dark. Based on the sound and rhythm of his breathing, she felt pretty sure Greer was awake, too, although she guessed the worries keeping him up were a little different than hers. She knew from past experience that if she apologized, he would too. Then he would tell her something he loved about her, something simple and ordinary — like how she made a certain face when she turned the page of a book — that she wouldn't expect. And the whole process of making up would allow them to talk about some of their problems, possibly even leading up to them making love, something they hadn't done yet in their new place.

But she couldn't bring herself to make the first move. She didn't know quite why since she usually didn't have much of a problem apologizing first if it meant getting Greer to open up. So, she continued to lie there, listening to Greer and thinking about the nightmare from the night before. In the dream she had wandered through a neighborhood much like their own in the sense that it was rundown and had lots of dead-end streets and alleyways. The strange thing was that it was always dark but people went about their regular business — walking to the post office, sitting on their front porch, strolling their baby — even though it was the middle of the night.

This thought made her uneasy, making her wonder what she would see if she got up and looked out the window. As the hours crept by that night, she just hoped the nightmare didn't become a permanent fixture in her life.

The next day Greer came with her on Duke's walk. It was late morning on a weekday, but Greer hadn't gone into work yet. They had both slept in late after not falling asleep till close to dawn. At first he had seemed irritated about the time, looking at the alarm clock as if it were a person that had seriously disappointed him. But then after his coffee he was making jokes about how nothing in the city was selling and any deal took forever to go through. "It's like the whole market is constipated or something." Greer covered his mouth with his hand and shook his head as if he regretted making the joke. Then, from somewhere in the other room, they heard Duke fart loudly. They both laughed.

When they were finished, the room seemed lighter. They smiled at each other from across the table. Penny felt the urge to reach out and hold his hand or apologize for the other day, but Greer spoke first.

"Let's do something together," he said. "The office can do without me today."

So they agreed to take Duke for a walk then come back and get cleaned up so they could go downtown. They decided to go into the forest because they knew the dog would enjoy it more. Neither of them said anything about the man with the beard. Neither of them said anything at all until they had been walking for a while. Then Greer mentioned something about a clothing store she liked.

"Maybe we could go there this afternoon," he said. "Haven't you been wanting some new jeans?"

She smiled.

"Yeah," she said. "But why don't we go somewhere we both enjoy?"

He stopped walking and gave her a quick pat on the butt.

"Don't you think I enjoy watching you try on new clothes?"

She smiled again and leaned in to kiss him. Their lips had barely touched when she felt Duke pulling at the leash. She finished the kiss early, coming away with just the faintest hint of maple syrup from the waffles Greer had eaten for breakfast.

"What's wrong?" Greer said.

She told him that Duke was ready to keep going.

"What if I'm not?"

There was a look on his face she hadn't seen in some time. It was a smile that instantly made him look younger and more confident, like a star athlete who knows he can have whatever girl he wants. Even though she had always been able to see through it, there was a part of her that still fell for it.

"Why don't you let Duke off his leash?" he said.

"This isn't the country, Greer."

He took the leash from her hand, pulled Duke in, and bent down to unclip the leash from the collar.

"I know that," he said. "I don't need a reminder."

She looked over at the dog. Duke had barely walked away from them. He was sniffing at some leaves that had collected at the base of a maple tree.

"See," Greer said as he took her hand. "He's fine."

Then he pulled her close and kissed her. For the next several minutes they kissed more than they had in the past few months. She was enjoying it, but she also would look at Duke out of the corner of her eye every few seconds. Every time Duke was still nearby, sniffing at more leaves. Eventually she relaxed more, letting her eyes close to appreciate the experience more. Before long she felt Greer's hands going inside her jeans. She looked around again to make sure she could see the dog and to make sure no one was watching; everything looked fine; the woods were quiet except for the sound of Duke pawing at leaves.

Greer whispered something about how he liked her jeans because they showed off her legs but weren't too tight he couldn't get his hand inside. She nodded and backed up against a tree to support her weight. She was surprised at how much she was enjoying the sense of danger that went along with what they were doing. She even started moving her hips along with the rhythm of his hand. Her sense of time and place fell away as she gave in to how her body felt. Only when Greer stopped touching her did she open her eyes.

"Why'd you stop?" she said.

"I heard something."

He said this as he took his hand from her pants. She felt a quick release of heat as if it were a breath forced out of her lungs. Before she had a chance to ask him what he heard, she noticed Duke wasn't nearby. In almost the same moment she heard a voice that sounded both close and far away, the way sound often is in dreams.

"It's him," she said, but Greer was already running toward where the noise was coming from.

She ran after her husband, the two of them almost tripping several times on tree roots hidden by leaves. Even though Greer didn't have much of a head start, he still got to Duke and the bearded man quicker than her. The bearded man was kneeling on the ground, one leg in front, the other in a posture that reminded her of how subjects knelt before a king. He was scratching Duke behind the ears and smiling.

He hardly had time to look up before Greer pushed him to the ground.

"Get the hell away from our dog!"

The man then said something Penny couldn't fully make out, something that must have pissed Greer off, because her husband shoved the man down again as he was trying to stand. She tried yelling the word stop, but the sound that came out sounded more like the surprised yelp of an animal than a recognizable word.

"I'm sorry," the man said. "I just miss her. I miss my girl."

The man started to rise again, so Penny stepped in between him and Greer. Greer stepped forward and she put a hand on his chest to stop him. She could feel how tight his muscles were, could feel each beat of his heart.

"Don't ever come near our dog again," Greer said.

Penny watched the man dust off his pants. He didn't look at her or Greer; Penny couldn't decide if she was grateful for this or not. A long moment passed where the man continued looking at his shoes, and then he turned to walk away. It wasn't until he was out of sight that she realized Duke wasn't nearby anymore.

She let go of Greer's chest and told him what she had noticed. In the same breath she almost said that Greer had scared him off by acting so crazy, but the words left her as quick as they had come.

"Let's split up," Greer said. "We'll find him faster that way."

She told him no.

"I don't want to be alone out here," she said, which was true. The thought of being by herself after what had just happened was worse than being with someone she was mad at. So, they started searching the woods, pausing every now and then to listen for the sound of leaves crunching or anything that would lead them to Duke. When they eventually caught up to their dog, he was walking side to side with his nose to the ground, as if he were trying to find the way back home.

She didn't sleep again that night. Moments after entering their apartment they had started fighting. She was mad at Greer for the way he had treated the man with the beard.

"You didn't need to hurt him," she said. "He didn't do anything."

Although she was still scared the man wanted to take Duke, she felt bad for him. He had a lot less going for him than she and Greer did.

"I don't understand you, Penny. You were the one that was so worried that guy would steal Duke. I was just sending him a message, and I'm pretty sure he won't come near us or our dog anymore."

Without waiting for a response, Greer moved toward the kitchen, where he opened and then slammed shut every cupboard.

"Jesus Christ," he said. "I can't find anything in this place."

She knew he was looking for booze but didn't offer to help. After opening every cupboard once more, Greer came back to the living room and started opening up boxes.

"I'm sick of not being able to find anything," he said.

"Why don't you do something about it?"

He shook his head, bent down to look into a box, and snatched up a bottle of scotch. He broke the seal and took a long pull. When he was finished he smiled, sat down at the table, and pointed at her.

"Why don't you start looking for a job like you said you would?"

She touched one hand to the middle of her forehead and held it there for a moment. "I don't like you very much when you drink," she said.

She had meant the words to come out angry and hurt but instead they sounded flat and tired, perhaps because she had already formed this opinion a while back. Greer looked at her without any expression at all. He wasn't blinking either. She couldn't explain it exactly, but she felt like the future of their entire relationship depended on what was said next and who spoke first.

"I think I should step out for a while," he said.

He spoke too quickly, almost as if he had been waiting to say those words. Before she could think of any response, he left the apartment, walking past her and Duke without saying goodbye. She sat there for a long time after he was gone, looking back and forth between Duke and the bottle of scotch. Later that night, as she looked at the clock and realized Greer wasn't coming home, she would regret not getting drunk enough to fall asleep.

The next morning she took the coffeemaker, a mug, and a magazine over to the other apartment. At first Duke just watched her without getting up, but after a while he followed her out the door of their apartment and into the other one. Along the way she kept up a mindless chatter that had the effect of calming her and irritating her all at once.

For the rest of the morning she sat in the other apartment, drinking coffee, reading magazines, and waiting for Greer. She understood that waiting for him instead of going about her day wasn't like her. At some point in her life she hadn't even believed in marriage; she used to believe that committing yourself, dedicating your life even, to someone else compromised who you were. Still, she loved her husband and just wanted some sense of order in her life. And if her old way of thinking held any truth, she had already lost part of herself, and there was no getting it back.

Around noon she got tired and decided to try to sleep again. But, as she was headed back to the other apartment, Duke started whining and pointing his head toward the street.

"You need your walk, don't you?" she said.

Duke barked once and continued looking out into the neighborhood.

"Wait here and I'll get your leash."

She left Duke on the porch and stepped inside. When she returned, Greer was standing there. He looked awful: his hair was greasy, his eyes were bloodshot, and he stank of booze and sweat.

"Jesus, Greer, where have you been?"

Before he could respond, she told him it didn't matter.

"We can talk later," she said. "I'm taking Duke for a walk now."

She clipped Duke's leash on and left the porch. She could hear Greer following her, but she didn't turn around.

"I want to talk to you, Penny," he said. "I want to apologize."

She stopped for a moment, looked him in the eye, and said, "For what?" She didn't know what she was hoping he'd say, but when he didn't reply after a minute, she kept walking. He did too, keeping pace with her and telling her about where he'd been last night.

"I wanted to make things right with you, so I found the guy that wanted Duke and apologized. His name's Ralph and he's a decent guy. We got to talking and ended up drinking at his place. It's just up the road."

"I think you should go home, Greer. Maybe get some rest."

He reached out and squeezed her wrist, not hard, but with enough force to make her stop walking so it didn't hurt her arm or shoulder.

"Just do this for me, Penny," he said. "I'm trying to make some changes for you."

He sounded desperate, and she couldn't bring herself to look him in the eye in case he looked even more pitiful. Duke looked up at her and then over at Greer, as if to say, "C'mon, I thought we were taking a walk."

"All right," she said. "But then you need to go home and get cleaned up."

They kept walking, going further up the street than she had been before. Greer stopped in front of a house with several boarded up windows and a front lawn littered with cigarette butts, wet newspapers, and what looked like bones from pork chops. Duke sniffed the bones, snapping each one up for a moment and then letting it fall out of his mouth.

On the porch were two people, Ralph and a teenage boy who had bad skin and wore ripped up black jeans. The kid was yelling and pointing his finger real close to Ralph's face.

"You fucking ripped me off!" he said. "That shit didn't even get me high."

Penny leaned over to Greer and whispered that they should leave. Probably calling the police would've made more sense, but she just wanted to be home: the lack of sleep was catching up to her and she felt the exhaustion in every part of her body.

"It's probably some sort of mistake," Greer said. "Ralph isn't a dealer."

Before she could respond, Greer was walking up to the porch. Neither Ralph nor the kid seemed to notice

Greer. Ralph was yelling now, saying he hadn't sold the guy anything.

"Get off my damn property!" Ralph said.

Greer walked up the last step to the porch, grabbed the kid's shoulder, and told him he needed to leave. Nearby, Duke bit down on one of the bones, making a scraping sound that startled her, causing her to look away from the porch. It looked like Duke was trying to swallow the bone, so she leaned over and knocked it from his mouth. When she looked up, Greer was on his knees, staring down at a knife that was stuck in his chest. There was a brief moment of silence, and then everyone, including herself, started screaming.

She ran to the porch, dropping Duke's leash in the process. The kid ran past her and down the street, tripping once on a section of uneven sidewalk. Ralph was leaning over Greer, repeating the same words over and over: "Why is this happening?"

It struck Penny that Greer — or even her — should've been the one saying that, not Ralph. Greer looked up at the two of them and, in a voice barely above a whisper, asked for someone to take the knife out. Ralph reached for the handle, but Penny grabbed his wrist and told him no. The wound didn't look too serious, and the knife didn't look too big, but she felt like a doctor should see it first.

"I'm calling 911," she said.

Almost immediately after she said this, she realized that the ambulance staff and doctors would probably think her husband was some kind of deadbeat based on how he looked today. Them seeing Ralph there, plus the condition of the house and yard, wouldn't do much to change that impression. Yet, like a lot of areas in her life lately, this seemed beyond her control. As she was taking out her cell phone, she noticed Duke had started running off, taking purposeful strides like he meant to get help. But even as

Penny dialed the numbers, she realized the help they needed would be a long time coming.

THE HOUSE NEXT DOOR

It was supposed to be an easy move. The Hamptons bought the house next door so they'd have a place that was really theirs. For years, Janet had lived in the home her husband had bought before they were married. Even though she did most of the decorating, she always felt the house carried a trace of the man Pete had been before they'd met. Over the years she had tried to not let this bother her. Lately, though, it seemed like her life had no direction. She needed to move forward. She needed something to call her own.

Her motivation increased whenever they were with their couple friends. Whenever Janet asked one of them how they were doing she'd get this reply: We're in a good place right now. Janet wanted to know what that felt like. All she had was a routine that consisted of watching game shows and old movies. She didn't ever consciously decide that moving could shake things up, but when the house next to theirs went up for sale she jumped at the opportunity.

It took her three weeks to get Pete on board. Even after he agreed to the idea he still didn't seem sure. At the closing, his skin looked a strange color. He wouldn't look at anyone. Once he left the room and didn't return for half an hour. When he returned there was a huge stack of papers he needed to sign and initial and, as he took up the pen, she thought he was going to vomit.

After it was all over she bought him a ginger ale from a vending machine and they held hands on their way outside. His hand was sticky but she held tight.

"We'll just bring over a few things everyday," Janet said as they left the realtor's office. "We won't even need a moving truck."

Pete bit down on his lip and smiled with just the corner of his mouth.

"How about we get some food to celebrate?" she said. "Anything you'd like."

He nodded but he still had that look which said he didn't know kindness from malice. They ordered pizza with all the toppings Pete liked. They also stopped at a convenience store and picked up beer, paper plates and napkins; Janet figured they could eat at their new place. She parked in their new driveway, turned off the engine, and unbuckled.

"We should get home," he said. "That pizza's probably getting cold."

A few days had gone by and Pete still hadn't set foot inside their new property. She, on the other hand, had been over a lot, bringing over a couple items each time. A stack of hand towels here, a couple plates there. Nothing that would be noticeable. Eventually, though, she'd need to do more and she was concerned how this would go over. Her friends told her to plan a romantic dinner at the new place. All you need to do is buy some champagne, light some candles, and fix his favorite food. He'll come around. When she told them how he wouldn't even come over for pizza, they got quiet. Oh, they said.

Over the next week Janet started bringing over the furniture. She didn't try to hide it either. Pete would be watching a movie and she'd walk right by him carrying an end table or chair. "I guess I'm going over to play house." His only response was to sink into the sofa. One night after dinner she started dragging the dining room table toward the front door.

"Here," Pete said, getting up from the sofa. "You can't get that alone."

They carried the table across both lawns and through the door of their new house. She expected to see him flinch or tense up as he entered, but all he did was keep his steady grip on the table.

"Where do you want it?" he said.

They set the table down to give their arms a rest.

"Where do you think it would look good?"

Pete looked around.

"It'll look the same no matter where it is."

"What's that supposed to mean, Pete?"

The furniture was all at the new place now. Her friends had helped move it while Pete was at work. Janet had wanted to at least leave the sofa and television, but Ruby had talked her out of it. Drastic times, babe. Janet knew that her friend was right. Pete had never come around on his own. He had always needed her to comfort him and make the change seem less overwhelming. But she had been doing this for years and was tired.

Once she had the new bedroom all set up, she went back to talk with Pete. She expected him to be upset, maybe start yelling at her, but he was just standing in the kitchen drinking a beer. She walked over to him and put her arm on his shoulder.

"Pete," she said. "It's time."

He drank off some of his beer, set it on the counter, and then ran his hand over the surface of one of the cabinets.

"I don't think I'm ready yet."

"You remember when you quit your job as janitor to make cabinets full time?"

He nodded.

"Aren't you happier now that you made the switch?"

He said he was, but that this was different.

"I've lived here a long time," he said. "I don't know anything else."

On her way out of the kitchen she told him that there was nowhere to sleep unless he liked the floor. He followed her to the front door. She stopped before stepping outside and turned to face her husband. He stared past her.

As she left the house she just told him she'd leave a light on for him.

A couple days passed before she saw Pete again. Janet was drinking coffee in the breakfast nook and looking out the window when Pete went by with the lawnmower. At first she simply waved as she would to any neighbor but, when she realized it was her husband, her hand froze. He saw her and stopped pushing the mower. He nodded. For a moment their eyes met. Then the breeze picked up, blowing grass clippings off of Pete's shirt, and he continued mowing.

A week later they pulled into their respective driveways at the same time.

"How've you been, Pete?"

"All right I suppose. Bought a new bed and sofa the other day but I don't care for them much."

"You can sleep in our bed, you know. I actually miss your snoring."

"I wish I could, Janet."

"I don't understand you," she said.

Pete looked down at the bushes, touching the spots that were growing uneven.

"Maybe I can't give you what you want."

She wanted to say that she wasn't asking for much, but she wasn't sure that was true.

A month went by. She figured it was just a phase they were going through. All couples had them. At night, lying in the bed she had shared with Pete for ten years, she thought about starting over: The thought of putting herself out there again after a divorce scared her. She knew building a new life was a lot of work, but then again, so was living with Pete.

All of these thoughts usually kept her awake. There was this urge to get up and look out the window to see if she could see Pete, an idea she knew was ridiculous because, for one, Pete went to bed at the same time every night and two, he always kept the curtains closed. So instead she'd just lay there and look at the ceiling or read a magazine.

She spent most of her time wondering what it looked like at Pete's. Part of her wondered if he had found the exact same furniture and then set everything up as it had been. Perhaps he was simply waiting for her to get tired of the new place and come back home. All she had to do was walk through the door and things would be more or less as they were. As the nights got colder and the maples started to turn, she had to admit this idea had some appeal.

Finally, she cracked. She went over one evening with some takeout and an old detective movie. The walk between the two houses seemed unbearably long. When she arrived at the door, she turned the handle but found it locked. She set the food down and got out her keys. For a moment she wondered if she had tried the new key by mistake, but when she compared the two, she realized Pete changed the locks. Now if she wanted to go inside, she would have to knock, as any neighbor would.

BEFORE THE SNOW FLIES

Jacy came home to the smell of burning sage and knew this meant that Hannah had come to stay again. The smell was thick, and the smoke seemed to enter through her skin rather than just her nose. It was supposed to be calming, but it always put her on edge. She also wondered if Hannah bundled in some little known plant found only in the deep woods, growing among poisonous mushrooms, wild ferns, lichen.

Like always when this happened, Jacy moved quickly through her home, dousing each bundle with water and then throwing them out the open windows. At one of the windows she paused for a minute to look at the garden. From where she stood the view was mostly of pokeweed but she knew underneath its pinkish stems grew more weeds: garlic mustard, Queen Anne's Lace, Creeping Charlie and several others which she had no name for. For weeks now she had meant to rip them out and reclaim the garden. She had no excuse for not getting to it either. Ever since she had failed out of college she didn't have many obligations.

Today would've been a perfect time to get outside, too: one of those warm autumn evenings where the air has a mildness that makes your whole body feel lighter. But now that her father's ex had come she had other problems to deal with.

After putting out all the sage, Jacy found herself both shivering and sweating, as if she had been struck by a sudden fever. She washed her face with a cool rag, put on one of her dad's old sweaters, and went to find Hannah.

She found her in the basement, in a small alcove where there were several wine racks and a couple massive shelves that had once been used for canning. The light from the room's one window was diffused with the oranges and reds of sunset. Hannah stood in the far corner of the room, nodding and mumbling something at such a pace that she couldn't understand one word. She yanked the string connected to the room's only light bulb, pulled her hands into the sleeves of the sweater, and said hello.

"This was your father's favorite place in the house," Hannah said, pointing to the window. "Something about how it got the last good light of the day."

Jacy nodded.

"I wish you wouldn't do this anymore," she said. "I don't think my dad's haunting this place."

Hannah moved over to the wine racks and, after methodically touching a few of the bottles, finally turned to look at her.

"I know that, child," she said. "The sage is to drive out the bad spirits so your dad's presence can come through.

Hannah pinched her eyebrows inward and whispered some more words Jacy didn't understand.

"Basically I'm trying to bring harmony to our house."

She started to say that it wasn't her house, but Hannah had turned to face the rack again where she slowly and deliberately went about rearranging them in what Jacy guessed was the order her dad put them in years ago. Each time Hannah came across an empty space she made a sound. When she was finished she turned to face her again.

"All this drinking won't help you deal with his passing, child."

Jacy started to explain that it wasn't just her drinking all the wine. Most weekends she had friends over and they'd spend most of the night hanging out, taking advantage of the extensive wine collection and the many unoccupied bedrooms. As she spoke, her words seemed to take on the feverish qualities she was feeling; every word came out rushed and blurred at the edges. When she was finished, Hannah took her hand and held it for some time. The smell of sage seemed to come back all at once.

"That won't help either."

The next morning she found Hannah in the garden, stooping low to yank out the various weeds. She worked with a grace and quickness that didn't seem possible for a woman in her late fifties. Hannah didn't look up even when she approached. For several minutes Jacy stood there, taking in the sight of the garden. Only a day ago she had thought that maybe it wasn't worth trying to save what she had planted. But now, in the brilliant morning light, the situation didn't look too bad; the tomato plants looked mostly ripe and the bugs hadn't done much damage to them; the peppers were almost ready too, and the rest of the vegetables seemed to be in good condition despite her neglect.

When she joined Hannah with the weeding she noticed there were two piles going; the larger one had only the vibrant colored pokeweed stalks while the other contained everything else.

"What are you doing with those," Jacy said, pointing at the larger pile.

Without stopping or looking up from her work Hannah said that she was going to make poke salad.

"Aren't those things poisonous?" Jacy said. "Even my dad wouldn't eat them."

At these words, Jacy remembered being a little girl and walking with her dad through the garden and then on to the forest that was also part of their property, land which now belonged only to her. Along the way he'd point out every species of plant they came upon and tell her whether it was edible or not. She was always surprised by how much you could eat, and also by how, despite the fact she never remembered many of the names, her dad would explain it all again with the same enthusiasm.

"They're actually delicious," Hannah said. "You just have to boil them enough times to get rid of all the toxins."

She then went on to explain how Native Americans also made medicine from the plant but most of those recipes have since been lost. Afterwards, Hannah stood up, brushed her hands on the faded jeans she wore, and looked at the nearby forest.

"I thought after we finished up with the garden we could hunt for some mushrooms," Hannah said. "And then for dinner I could make Coq Au Vin."

Jacy set down the Queen Anne's Lace she had been ripping out and turned to face Hannah.

"You know I won't go into those woods. Besides," she said. "That's not why I came out here. I came out here to tell you that you need to leave after today."

She spoke quickly, with her hands pressed hard into her pockets. For some time Hannah continued looking off at the forest where a few of the maples were just starting to turn. Jacy expected her to say something like, It's been a year since we found him there. You're going to have to go back sometime. But Hannah said nothing like this and after a couple minutes Jacy repeated herself.

"Can I ask why?"

There were any number of reasons she could've given her, all of them valid, but she had used them before. And always Hannah would find some way to undermine her position or else make Jacy feel guilty for turning her out of the place she'd lived in for nearly a decade. Today, though, she decided to go another route.

"I met somebody and I want him to move in here," Jacy said.

The somebody was a guy she had met at one of the parties she'd thrown recently. Although they'd only hung out several times, it felt more serious than other relationships. Probably, she guessed, because he was a good bit older than her and his maturity added some gravity to their relationship. It had, however, been at least a week since they'd spoken. Hannah opened her mouth to say something but Jacy cut her off.

"By us, I mean just him and I."

Hannah sighed and looked over at the house.

"Well," she said. "I'd at least like to meet him. Why don't you bring him over for dinner tonight?"

Jacy pulled one more weed and then clasped her hands together. Even though she'd only been in the garden a short time they felt sweaty and raw.

"He's working tonight," she said. "So it'll have to be tomorrow."

Hannah nodded and then said something about going to pick the mushrooms by herself. Once again Hannah looked at the house with a feeling that Jacy guessed was nostalgia. The way she sucked on her lower lip and raised her eyes suggested she was traveling back to some distant memory, perhaps one that didn't even involve her dad or the years Hannah had spent with him.

"I'll finish up here," Jacy said.

Without nodding or saying anything, Hannah turned and started off for the woods, measuring her steps carefully as the earth dipped past the garden's edge. Jacy felt like there was more to say but couldn't bring herself to follow Hannah's path.

Her boyfriend — she used this term only because she didn't know what else to call him — sounded friendlier on the phone than she'd expected. He said that he was surprised she'd called.

"I've tried," she said. "I left messages too."

Her face got warm as she remembered the rambling messages, some of them made late in the evenings after she'd lost herself in wine.

"Sorry," he said. "I've been out of the house a lot lately."

He went on to say that he thought he had told Jacy he'd be gone for a while and would call her when he returned. He sounded impatient, like he was talking to a child.

"I don't remember that," she said.

In her voice Jacy recognized some of Hannah's defiance or whatever word it was that described how Hannah could turn a situation around and make the other person feel like they were at fault. She wished she could take it back. She waited several moments and, when the silence became too much, said, "Well, I don't have anything going today if you wanted to get together." At first it was quiet on his end and she wondered if he was still there. She was about to hang up when he finally spoke.

"Sure," he said. "Let's meet somewhere."

She met him at a café in town. He had arrived before her and was already standing in line, chatting easily with the college age girl working the register. For several minutes she just stood there watching him, this man she barely knew yet was considering living with. There was a natural energy in his every movement that made whatever he was talking about seem important. Part of it was his body language, the quick gestures that punctuated his thoughts and the air of reflection he took on when he was listening to others. A lot of it, though, was simply the timbre of his voice. Half the time she found herself focusing on this sound rather than what he had actually said. It was his voice which had initially drawn Jacy to him and now hearing it directed at another girl, perhaps even one of his students at the local college, made her jealous.

She was about to interrupt his conversation when he came her way carrying their drinks.

"I got you an espresso," he said. "You like those, right?"

He was right, although she had no memory of saying this to him and they had never hung out anywhere except for her place. She nodded and followed as he walked past her and out the door where he set the drinks down at a table. The chairs were positioned so that they would be sitting next to each other rather than across. She waited for a moment to see if he would move the seats, but he sat down right away, brushing against her hip in the process. His confidence now almost made her forget his shame as he buttoned his pants the last time they'd been together.

"How's the garden?" he said.

"Fine, I guess. I haven't been out there as much as I should. I probably missed my chance to plant a crop to harvest in winter."

He placed one hand to his forehead like he was thinking of something. Then he closed his eyes for a moment. When he opened them he was smiling.

"What if you used a cold frame?" he said. "Didn't you say that you had some of those lying around?"

Her dad had constructed them years ago from old screen doors. They were basically miniature greenhouses and required very little work. For some reason, though, they had ended up in the basement, and she hadn't taken the trouble of moving them upstairs and out into the garden.

"I guess I could," she said. "It might be too late already, and it'd be more work than I care for right now."

In these words Jacy recognized the same attitude that had caused her to flunk out of college. The overall lack of motivation was something she was trying to work on. Her goal right now was to get a job before winter came. Elliot smiled, took a sip of his coffee, and then reached for her hand.

"I could come out and help," he said. "I don't have much going on right now since I'm technically still on sabbatical. Plus, you said the house needed some repairs and I could take care of those too."

The meaning of his words seemed to hang thick between them and she felt the sudden need to let go of his hand.

"What do you think?" he said.

Jacy looked again at the scene around her. No one was looking at them but it felt as though they had been recently and had just now turned back to what they were doing, their raised books and coffee mugs covering up their silent laughter at her situation. When she turned back to look at Elliot it was as though he wouldn't look at her either; he was looking around absently as if the answer she gave didn't have much importance. She drank her espresso in one swallow and the quick rush of heat brought on the same feverish feeling she'd had the other day.

"Why don't you come for dinner tonight?" she said. "Then we'll see what happens."

She decided not to tell Elliot that Hannah would be there for dinner. In previous conversations Jacy had told him about Hannah and her strange ways — the burning sage, the teas she liked to brew up using roots and leaves from the forest, the way she showed up suddenly and ordered Jacy around — but he had never seemed impressed by the woman's behavior or concerned about the effect they had on her.

"One time I woke in the middle of the night and she was sitting in a chair next to my bed. I thought it was an intruder at first and nearly had a heart attack. Now every night I go to bed wondering if she'll do it again. A person can't live like that."

All Elliot had said when she told him this story was that Hannah probably cared for Jacy more than she realized. That's not a bad thing, he'd said. Now, though, he'd realize that Hannah was a little unbalanced and he'd have to help get rid of her.

When she got home her mind was racing from all these thoughts plus the espresso. There was still another hour before Elliot would come and she felt a sharp impatience that she had to wait so long to get her new life started. She decided to work off some of her energy in the garden. When she got there the first thing she noticed was the missing pile of pokeweed. She imagined Hannah in the kitchen, boiling the stalks and leaves for the third and last time before putting together a salad. At first Jacy was mad. There was no way she would eat something which every sane person knew was poisonous. She headed inside to tell Hannah not to serve the dish, practicing how she'd phrase it as she walked. But as she ran the lines over in her mind something happened: she began to hear Hannah's voice responding to her order. Your father was the healthiest man I knew. He did everything he was supposed to and he still died way before he should've. These words seemed to carry the implicit idea that just the simple process of waking up each morning carried with it some risks.

By the time Jacy reached the house she decided not to say anything. She even grew to like the idea that the three of them would all share the same risk by eating the poke salad. So when she walked through the back door and into the kitchen all she did was say a quick hello to Hannah and went upstairs to clean up.

Elliot showed up exactly at the time she'd told him but she didn't come downstairs right away. Instead, she waited around so he could get a taste of weird. Jacy left her bedroom door open and stood listening to their conversation. She expected it either to be filled with awkward gaps or else for Hannah to talk enough for both of them. But after a couple minutes she had mainly heard Elliot and his pleasant baritone, the voice that probably drew more female students to his lectures than what was normal for Ancient Roman History. When Jacy heard Hannah laughing, she decided it was time to come downstairs.

She found them in the kitchen where Hannah was asking what type of wine he preferred.

"He likes a Cabernet," Jacy said. "Elliot, why don't you help me find one in the cellar?"

Hannah wouldn't start the meal without giving a toast. First, though, she made a big deal out of refilling Jacy's glass — she drank her first while they were still in the kitchen — and saying how maybe it wasn't such a good idea that her dad let her try the stuff at such a young age.

"He was a great father," Hannah said. "I suppose it would've been hard not to spoil your only daughter. Anyhow, I just want to welcome Elliot to this house. I think it's great that Jacy found someone, especially someone a little older who can hopefully give her some direction in life. That's something Jonas would've wanted. He always said . . ."

Up till now Hannah had been looking at Jacy but as she broke off she turned to look at some photographs on a nearby table. They were all of Jacy's father as a younger man. Some were even publicity photos which had appeared alongside articles praising his commitment to the environment. Hannah's face, while looking at them, still contained the enthusiasm of her speech, as if she was just waiting for this moment to pass before she continued talking. The only gesture which revealed her sadness was in the hand she used to hold her wine glass; every few seconds she would lower it a degree or two, so that after a few minutes it nearly touched the table.

"Anyhow," Hannah said. "I guess we should enjoy what we've got while we've got it."

Everyone at the table touched glasses. Afterwards, Hannah described the food she was about to serve. When she got to the bowl of poke salad she skipped Jacy's plate and only served Elliot and herself.

"People have been eating this for years," Hannah said. "But our girl here is afraid it's poisonous."

Jacy wanted to say something in her defense, only she couldn't think of anything which wasn't either paranoid or childish, both qualities which lately she feared she possessed.

"I like things that are bad for me," Elliot said. "The worse the better actually."

It took considerable effort for Jacy not to watch where he was looking as he said the last part. It was even more difficult not to say something like, Well, then you've come to the right place.

Jacy could hear Elliot moving around in her room as she brushed her teeth. She had been in the bathroom getting ready for a while now and the longer she took the more nervous she was to return. Their previous attempt at sex had not gone well. They had fooled around a bit but never made love. At first he hadn't seemed nervous at all, though it was their first time; he went inside her right away and placed both hands on her lower back. When he started moving, though, he was so cautious and there didn't seem to be any logic to the impossibly slow rhythm. It all made her feel disconnected from what was happening, and the longer it went on the creepier it made her feel. She ended up saying something along the lines of, Would you just fuck me already! It surprised them both and even after she apologized he wasn't able to continue.

All of her former lovers had fallen into one of two categories: men who cared little for her pleasure and simply raced for the main event or men who, according to her, were insecure and therefore devoted themselves to her needs first with a focused intensity she didn't think she was capable of repaying. Neither type of man was ideal but at least she knew what to expect. She didn't know what to do with Elliot, and it affected more than the bedroom. Up until a week ago she'd felt his age, along with the fact he had a career which had given him an advantage in their relationship. Or if not an advantage, he at least played the role of senior partner, the one who had more control over the direction they'd take as a couple. The sudden shift had her confused.

When she finally entered the room she found Elliot sitting on the edge of her bed. The cuffs of his shirt were rolled back but otherwise he was fully dressed whereas she had changed into the loose fitting t-shirt she typically wore to bed. Other than this, all that covered her body was her underwear.

Jacy walked toward the bed, pausing halfway to see what kind of effect she was having on him. He was looking right at her but not in a way that suggested he wanted her. She quickly got into bed and pulled the covers halfway up her body.

"I think I like Hannah," he said. "She's kind of an amateur historian, don't you think?"

He had turned to face her but spoke as if to a classroom of people. The tone of his question seemed to want a brief nod from the audience rather than a real answer. She gave him neither.

"I like her stories too," he said.

He went on to say that his favorite ones were about Hannah living in the nearby woods, which was something Jacy had been unaware of till earlier in the evening. Already Jacy felt troubled by the image of her out there in the woods, sleeping in lean-tos, eating strange plants, and tracking deer over the frost covered earth. She was sure these thoughts would twist and distort themselves as she slept.

"I like her fine," Jacy said. "I just don't want her living in my house anymore or out in the woods."

She realized her tone had something of the impatience from the last time they'd been in her room. He nodded, said that he understood.

"Let's not talk about her right now," she said. "Why don't you get in bed with me?"

He nodded again, slower this time, and then set about taking off his clothes. It seemed to take him forever and with each article he removed Jacy grew more anxious.

Her heart beat like it did whenever she smelled the burning sage. She'd never been this nervous with a guy before, not even for her first time, although with that boy the whole thing had happened so fast there wasn't much time to be nervous. By the time he came to bed her chest felt so tight she knew she would have to relax quite a bit if anything was going to happen.

Elliot took her hand and held it between both of his for a long moment.

"Thanks for giving me another chance," he said.

He then moved forward to kiss her. She shut her eyes and willed herself to relax. But when their lips touched she found that his mouth stayed shut. One dry kiss and then he rolled over, said goodnight, and turned off the lamp. Only a minute ago she had felt closed off but now she felt a little bothered and didn't know what to do about it. She could've tried to start something but it didn't seem like what he wanted right now. She could've kicked him out of bed but this seemed too much like the impulsive reaction a child would have. After a minute of weighing her options, Jacy curled up against the warmth of his body but told herself it was only as protection from the dreams she might have.

In the morning Jacy woke up alone. She had no idea what time he had gotten out of bed although the rich, musky smell clinging to the sheets made her think he had at least stayed part of the night. After a minute of wondering what it would've been like waking up with him, Jacy got up, showered, and went downstairs.

The kitchen smelled of coffee, eggs, mushrooms, and herbs. A couple of plates and mugs had been washed and placed in the drying rack. In the refrigerator was a container which held the ingredients for omelettes, neatly portioned out for one. Jacy looked at it for a second but didn't think it would sit well considering the amount of wine she'd had. Instead she poured herself some coffee from what was left in the pot, put on a sweater, and went outside.

She found Elliot and Hannah in the garden. They had apparently located all of the cold frames from the basement and hauled them out here. Now they were discussing where they should be placed and what they should plant in each one. Neither of them seemed to notice her until she spoke.

"Isn't it too late in the season for this," Jacy said. "It's already October."

Hannah looked at her in a way that suggested annoyance.

"It might be," Hannah said. "But we don't have anything to lose by trying. Besides, once the plants start growing they'll be fine in these even after the snow flies."

Jacy remembered her father using this expression except he had always said before the snow flies. As in, "Jacy, could you help me plastic the windows today? I want to get this done before the snow flies." Growing up, there was always a huge list of chores she needed to help with so they could be ready for winter and every year she dreaded them because it meant time she wasn't able to hang out with her friends. Yet at the same time she looked forward to winter and the way her dad was more relaxed. In the evenings they would eat venison stew, drink a little wine, and then read books or watch movies together. Those nights held some of her favorite memories of her dad.

"How'd you sleep?" Elliot said.

"Fine," she said.

Even though she didn't ask him the same question, he went on to explain that he slept all right considering he wasn't familiar with the environment yet. He also went on to say how beautiful she looked while she was sleeping.

"You have this look of expectancy about you that reminds me of how kids look when they're pretending to sleep."

Both Elliot and Hannah smiled at her. Jacy might've enjoyed this conversation if it had been spoken in a more intimate setting but out here, with Hannah present, she couldn't help but feel there was a mocking undertone to his words.

"Elliot," Jacy said. "I thought you and I could go into town this afternoon. Maybe see a movie or something." As she waited for his response, Jacy drank some of her coffee.

"How about tomorrow?" he said. "Hannah wanted to take me out into the woods today You should come too."

Jacy drank the rest of her coffee then looked out at the woods. On some days, especially mild autumn evenings, she did miss taking hikes. However, the second she set foot in the woods she felt what she could only describe as a premonition, a feeling that, just like her dad, she would die in the woods.

"Has she ever told you what happened out there?" Jacy said. "Because, if she has, you wouldn't ask me to come along."

Without waiting for a response she started walking away from them, away from a life that, in recent months, seemed to move forward without her control. As she made her way through the garden she felt like giving everything up: the woods, the garden, the house, all the things her father had left her. The combination of money and land from his estate was too much for her to handle at the age of twenty two. Some days she felt it was somehow rotting her values, her outlook on life, while other days she felt her moods could be blamed on her dad's recent death.

By the time she neared the garden's edge, Jacy could hear Elliot calling out to her. She couldn't make out the words yet, but she could hear the concern in his voice. She kept walking. Eventually he caught up with her and said her name in a near breathless way that made her stop.

"Hannah told me what happened," he said. "And I'm sorry."

He nodded and took her hand. The color in his cheeks and the work clothes he wore didn't seem to fit with his styled hair or the careful way he wouldn't look her directly in the eye.

"We can go to town if you want," he said. "Just let me get cleaned up and then we'll leave."

She nodded and he squeezed her hand. Together they walked inside and through the kitchen where the smell of breakfast still lingered. Jacy was feeling a little better about her life until they got upstairs and passed the room where Hannah stayed. Not only were there no suitcases packed, but there were picture frames on the nightstand and stems of Queen Anne's Lace in a small, cut-glass vase Hannah had received as a gift from Jacy's dad. Jacy let go of Elliot's hand and said, "She's never going to leave here."

They tried making love again that night. Jacy made sure neither of them drank more than a glass of wine at dinner so she could be sure it wasn't a factor. More importantly, though, she tried moving slower, since it seemed like what he wanted. They spent a long time kissing before they even undressed. Then, after they finally took off their clothes, he went between her legs with his hand. She was surprised at his boldness and how good it felt. She could've finished this way but still felt the need to have him inside, not because it would necessarily feel better but because she had the overwhelming need to see something through to the end. So, reluctantly, she took away his hand and climbed on top of him.

There was an intense moment of warmth as she lowered herself until he was in all the way. She shut her eyes to fully enjoy it and then started moving.

"Jacy," he said, his voice strained. "Don't."

She thought it was because he was worried about protection or perhaps finishing too soon.

"It's all right," she said, in a way she hoped conveyed both that she was on the pill and that it didn't matter how long he lasted.

But it wasn't all right. As she moved up he slipped out. She tried to start over but the second she felt him she knew it wasn't happening. Before she could say anything he was apologizing.

"I didn't think that would happen," he said. "But we don't have to be done."

She had rolled off of him and curled up with her knees pressed together. He started kissing her neck and then she felt his hand on her thigh.

"Don't," she said.

She moved away from him, away from the heat their bodies had created. Without really thinking about it, she got out of bed and walked over to the window. There wasn't much moonlight. She couldn't even make out the edge of the woods, but she felt its dim presence in the night.

"I don't understand," she said. "You like me, don't you?"

He responded quickly but she didn't turn to face him.

"Of course I do," he said. "I think we might really have something together."

Hearing his voice without seeing his face made him seem younger somehow.

"Then what's the problem?"

He sighed loudly and, as if in response, she shivered. The house seemed colder than usual and Jacy wondered if it was because Hannah had left some windows open, a habit which Hannah kept up no matter how cold it was outside. She wanted to get back in but wasn't ready to be near him again.

"I'm not sure what it is exactly," he said. "But none of it's your fault."

He went on to explain that he had recently been involved with a college student. The relationship ended badly, and basically resulted in a forced sabbatical. From this explanation, Jacy had only a vague understanding of how these events affected their relationship. It felt like she had been handed just a few puzzle pieces with the expectation that she needed to create the complete picture.

From outside, she heard some noises that sounded like animals running; first there was a scrabbling noise like paws against the stone patio and then a rush of crackling leaves. She tried looking for whatever had made the noise but saw nothing. It had been this way when she found her dad in the woods. After accepting the fact he was dead, she tried to say a few words to him but all around her she kept hearing branches stir, leaves crunch, air being displaced by the quick movements of whatever creatures lived nearby. At any moment she expected a whole menagerie of animals to surround the little clearing where her dad lay slumped against a fallen oak. In the end, she couldn't control her imagination and took off to find Hannah. When they returned, the clearing was very still and, although her dad didn't look much different, his body seemed to be part of the decomposition that was going on all around them. Even when Hannah asked if she needed a moment alone she wasn't able to find any words for him.

"Do you believe me?" Elliot said.

The sudden, pleading nature of his voice made her turn to face him.

"You have to give me something else to go on."

She meant this but there wasn't much force to her words. Mainly she just wanted a reason to get back into bed.

"I don't know if I can explain it right. Especially since I don't understand it fully myself."

Jacy turned to look out the window once more before coming to bed.

"I think I can relate to that," she said.

That night she dreamt she had gone into the woods. Usually this dream consisted of her wandering around until she came upon her dad's body and either ran away screaming or else laid down next to him in the frost hardened grass, holding close to his body even though it seemed to draw the warmth right out of her. But now the content of her nightmare had changed. She was still walking around the woods but not because she was looking for her dad. Instead she was simply trying to find a way out. Yet no matter how far she traveled in any direction there was nothing but trees, giant trees whose trunks appeared blurry to her, the leaves lacking the distinct shapes which normally would've revealed what species they were. Gradually she realized the woods were a sort of purgatory, a place she was forced to roam as penance for a sin she had no knowledge of committing.

Jacy woke up from this dream feeling calm, resigned to whatever her life might bring. It was an emotion she hadn't felt since her dad had been alive and even then it only happened when they were out hiking together. She tried holding on to this feeling as she got dressed, left Elliot sleeping in her bed, and went downstairs.

Even though it was before dawn, Hannah was awake. Jacy found her sitting at the kitchen table drinking a bitter smelling tea.

"I made some coffee too," Hannah said. "I know you don't care for the tea I make."

"Not now," Jacy said.

Jacy found her dad's sweater by the back door and put it on. She also put on the pair of shoes she wore when she was working in the garden. Hannah stood up, walked over to her, and laid a hand on her shoulder.

"Do you want me to come with you?"

Jacy shook her head.

"I'll go alone."

She made for the back door before she could change her mind.

Outside the air was cold, but not cold enough that she could see her breath. Jacy tucked her hands into the sleeves and started walking. She didn't stop in the garden to check on any of the plants or look at the cold frames which Hannah and Elliot had set up. She also didn't look back at the house or in any direction except toward the woods in front of her.

Still, after walking for a few minutes, she hadn't made it very far. She was shivering too, and she knew that if she didn't do something she'd end up turning around, going back inside, and climbing into bed with a man she didn't know.

She ran, and as she picked up speed all her thoughts fell away. There was only the cold air against her face and the crunch of her feet against the hard ground. But when she reached the woods she stopped abruptly short.

For several moments she just stood there, catching her breath and taking in the crisp smell of the forest. The memories it brought to mind came quick but disappeared each time she exhaled. When she took her next step, she wanted to believe the moment would somehow give her the power to take control of her life or, at the very least, give her the strength to get rid of Hannah and Elliot and, more importantly, visit the place where her father had died. It all seemed within her reach.

But it was just a step, and before continuing on she couldn't resist taking a look back toward the house. She hoped someone was watching.

THE NOISE

He woke his kids up at night when he heard the noise. His boy woke easy, but the girl took some rousing; he had to tug her arm until she practically fell from her bed. He led them, bleary eyed and sour breathed, out of their rooms and down the stairs.

"It's happening again," he said.

Then he slid open the patio and motioned them outside.

"Do you hear it?"

The kids took long, ragged breaths and listened while their dad listened too, cocking his head at different angles to better hear the noise: it was a man's voice coming over a loudspeaker, he thought. The loudspeaker seemed to be coming from far away, and the words weren't distinct, but it sounded like the man was saying different names.

"I guess so," the kids mumbled. "Can we go back to sleep now?"

He shook his head.

"No, no, don't you hear it? They're saying her name."

The boy stood up straighter now.

"Whose name?"

"Your ma's, son. Can't you hear it?"

The man pointed toward the sound so hard his elbow locked up. The boy shook his head.

"That could be anyone's name. I'm going back to sleep, dad."

Before he reached the patio, he turned around and told his dad to get some sleep, too.

"Sure, sure," the dad said. "I'll go upstairs in a minute." But his kids were inside already, shuffling upstairs, back to dreams that would take them to a place less strange than this. The father walked to the edge of the yard and stood underneath a hackberry tree. He listened to the loudspeaker voice drone on, saying the same name again and again. *Leslie Peterson ... Leslie Peterson ... Leslie Peterson.* It was her name. He knew it in his heart. She was at the factory working third shift a mile or so down the road, but she might as well have been worlds away: she wouldn't see him anymore, even when he dropped off the kids, and she hung up whenever he tried to phone.

Why were they saying her name so much? Was she in trouble? Did she forget to show up for work? And why could he hear the loudspeaker so well lately? He shook his head and looked up at the leaves of the hackberry tree: all of the leaves had big warty bubbles. He had mentioned it to Leslie once, but she hadn't shown much interest. *The tree is fine, Troy. It's still standing, isn't it?* And when he hadn't responded, she threw in another barb: *Since when do you care about trees anyway?*

He tried to swallow but found his mouth dry. It was quiet now, except for the breeze rattling the leaves and a cricket chirping. He headed to the patio door but found it locked. He cursed silently and rummaged among some chipped flower pots until he located the spare.

In the kitchen, he drank two fingers of whisky at the sink and chased it with what remained of a beer he'd opened at dinner. He went to the bedroom and closed the window despite the heat. He got back into bed but got out before even touching the pillow. He grabbed two cotton balls from the medicine cabinet and stuffed them in his ears. Before getting back into bed, he turned on an old black and white television Leslie had always tried to get him to throw out.

In the morning, he fetched the paper from the porch wearing only his boxers and an undershirt. His daughter stood up from the table as he entered the kitchen. She dumped half a bowl of cereal into the sink and left the room.

"I was about to get dressed," he said, but she was already gone.

He heated some water in the microwave, scooped in some instant coffee, and stirred it up. While he blew on the coffee, he opened up the paper. He skimmed through the pages looking for any news about the factory where Leslie worked or about Leslie herself. Nothing. He checked to see what day it was, saw that it was a Tuesday, and flipped to the classifieds. There were a couple openings for maintenance workers, but he didn't feel like grabbing a pen, so he closed the paper.

The clock on the stove said nine thirty, which meant his daughter should've been in school. He called upstairs.

"Kelsey Marie!"

In response, he heard a radio turn on. He left his coffee on the table and walked upstairs. He stood at her door, about to knock, when he heard a song he liked: "Dead Flowers" by The Rolling Stones.

"Kelsey," he said, speaking her name softly now. "Didn't you miss school yesterday?"

Without opening the door, she said, "Yeah, and I'm not going today either."

Last he knew, she was failing at least two classes and had missed plenty of days. She had quit doing her chores some time back, too. In this way, she was nothing like Leslie, who had always been a workaholic. This made him both happy and disappointed.

"Well," he said. "Try and get some rest then."

He started walking away but stopped before he reached his room.

"And try to tackle some of your homework."

He came home late that night. He was drunk and happy, a rare combination. For the past several hours, he had been winning hand after hand at poker night with the guys. He usually played terribly when he was hammered, but for some reason everything had clicked: the cards went his way all night, and his usual tell, one he could never figure out, had apparently disappeared because all his bluffs worked. Once inside, he grabbed a beer from the fridge and sat down at the kitchen table. While he drank, he counted up his winnings: seventy three dollars, enough for a couple weeks worth of groceries. His bank account was nearly empty, but he had already paid the mortgage, water bill, and electric bill with the last of his unemployment checks.

He was good for a little while, but he needed to make a move. Fuck the maintenance jobs and janitor positions. He was lonely as hell as it was; he didn't need some job where he was by himself all day, just him and his stupid thoughts of Leslie. He was a people person, a problem solver. Who knows, maybe he would even go back to school and earn himself a degree. The thought of sitting in some classroom set him on edge some, but maybe not in a bad way.

He drank the rest of his beer while staring at the dirty dishes in the sink. Kelsey was supposed to have washed them earlier. He still could picture the look of bored disgust as she had said, *Why can't we just get a dishwasher like normal people?* After setting his empty bottle next to the sink, he grabbed another bottle, the last one, from the fridge and headed upstairs. As he approached Kelsey's door, he tried to stay calm.

From inside, he heard the radio playing a different station than the other day. The song's bleak keyboards and violins scratched and tore at his buzz.

"Kelsey," he said, quietly at first, then a bit louder.

He gripped the doorknob and turned it slowly, trying not to make any noise. He remembered checking on her when she was a baby, how cautious he was even though she could sleep through anything, including the time when construction workers were jackhammering practically outside her window during an afternoon nap.

He stepped through the open door and into the room. It was nearly pitch dark; only the red light from the clock radio cut through the blackness. The depressing song ended, and the radio went to a commercial. In the brief moment of silence, he listened for Kelsey's breathing but heard nothing. As his eyes adjusted to the darkness, he watched the bed for movement. Again, nothing. He crossed the room and touched the covers, but his fingers sank into the mattress.

"Shit," he said.

He turned the light on and confirmed what he already knew: the room was empty. There wasn't any note on her desk. He left her room and stood at his son's door. Within seconds, he could hear him snoring. Troy went downstairs and checked the kitchen and living room for a note.

"Shit shit shit!"

He immediately thought of what Leslie would say if she knew he didn't know where their daughter was. He stood in the kitchen for a minute trying to figure out what to do. For a second, he considered waking Brian, but the two of them rarely spoke anymore. There was the possibility she was at a friend's house, but this too seemed unlikely since she spent most of her time alone. He could call Leslie to see if Kelsey was there, but unless Kelsey answered, he would have to admit to being a bad parent.

O.K., think for a minute, Troy. You can figure this out.

He sat down on the couch and held on to his head with both hands as if to steady himself. He wished he hadn't drank those last beers; he wished he hadn't drank too much when Leslie was around; he wished he didn't .... He stood up and shook his head. The room spun for a moment but then returned to normal. From the kitchen he grabbed a drink of water and headed outside. As he passed the table, he eyed the small pile of bills; he grabbed a few, along with his keys, and left the house.

Outside, fireflies lit up the front yard. The front grass needed mowing, and the porch crumbled a bit as he walked on it. Before he was even out of his yard he heard the voice again: *Leslie Peterson, Leslie Peterson, Leslie Peterson.* This time he was sure. He sprinted down the block and down a small hill leading into Sycamore Park. It was the quickest way to the factory and Leslie's apartment. He had no idea what he would do when he got to the factory or her apartment, so for the moment he focused on running.

There were no streetlights once he entered the park. The occasional headlights from the nearby road cut through the row of sycamores lining the park, and a few houses in the distances had lights on, but otherwise it was hard to make things out except for the bleachers by the ball diamond, the basketball hoops and the pavilion. He ran as fast as he could, moving toward the noise. The voice on the loudspeaker seemed to grow in volume, only now the man was saying other names, too.

He continued on a ways but stopped at the nearby pavilion when he ran out of breath. As he leaned against the wall and listened, it occurred to him maybe he had been wrong about them saying Leslie's name. He shook his head and tried to breathe normal. The back of his throat burned and his legs ached. He stumbled around the pavilion until he found the drinking fountains. After taking a long drink and splashing his face, he kept walking.

The loudspeaker was still going, but he wasn't paying much attention now. He focused on what he would say to Leslie if she would open her door to him. *I still love you. I'm going to make some changes. I don't know where Kelsey is right now.* Nothing sounded good; he figured the right thing would come to him when he saw her face.

At the far edge of the park he heard some noises from off in the bushes. For a second, it sounded like someone was hurt, but he quickly realized it was a woman moaning. He followed the sound over to a row of bushes.

Crouching low, he pulled back some branches and looked through. Although it was dark, the light from a nearby house allowed him to see two people on the ground. The girl was on the bottom, and the guy on top, jeans pulled down to his ankles. He guessed they were both young, but it was hard to tell. The girl had her palms flat on the ground instead of wrapped around his back; her hands were small like Kelsey's. For all he knew, it could have been her. He knew it probably wasn't, but once the thought got into his head, he couldn't shake it.

He crept along the bushes, the dew soaking his pant cuffs, hoping to get a better look at them. The loudspeaker man was still talking, but Troy could still hear the man in the bushes grunting and his movements getting quicker. It was quiet for a moment, and then he heard the girl speak: "Take it out of me already."

Her voice had the same bored and sour edge Kelsey's did, but he wasn't sure it was her. Up ahead there was a space in the bushes, so he crawled to it, trying to be as quiet as possible. He heard the guy zip his pants and laugh. The girl didn't say or do anything. He hung back from the opening a bit while the guy walked away. Troy studied the guy as he walked: he was definitely young, no more than eighteen or so, and he was skinny the way a lot of junkies were. Troy tried to remember his face, so he could find him and beat the shit out of him if he had just screwed his daughter.

Troy got off the ground and stood in the opening so he could see the girl better. She was standing now, too, brushing some leaves off of her skirt. Her hair was too long to be Kelsey. He took a long, deep breath and started to turn around.

"If you're looking for a piece," a voice said. "I'm all done with her."

Troy turned around to see the teenager smiling at him.

110

"She wasn't great, but she didn't cost too much either."

The kid laughed once then walked away. Troy turned around to see the girl had moved closer to him. She was young, but not as young as he had thought: probably at least in her twenties. She wasn't bad looking, although it was hard to tell too much in the dark.

"I'm still working," she said. "If you're up for anything."

He didn't move or nod or blink or anything. It was the first time in recent memory a woman had said anything to him that wasn't filled with hatred, disgust, or boredom. She moved closer and touched him through his jeans. He opened his mouth but nothing came out.

With one hand she kept touching him, and with the other she felt his pockets, first his back pocket and then his front. She pulled the money out and nodded. He tried to nod, too, but all he could focus on was what her hand was doing. A few seconds later she was pulling down his jeans. He stepped out of them and let her pull him to the ground.

The loudspeaker was still going, almost like a radio in the next room, but now he thought they were saying Leslie's name again. The girl tugged at her skirt until it was above her waist, and then she started guiding him in. He was vaguely aware he didn't have a rubber on. He thought about asking if she had one or telling her to stop, but instead he asked if she heard the noise.

"You mean that loudspeaker? she said. "Yeah, I hear it."

He was inside her now. She was slicker than anything he'd felt, and he realized it might've been from what the other guy had done.

"What's he saying?" he said.

She grinded her hips against his.

"It sounds like he's saying Leslie Peterson."

He grabbed hold of her hips and pumped harder.

111

"That's my wife," he said.

He wanted to say more, a lot more, but as was the case with all the women in his life, it didn't seem there was much more he could say that would matter.

LOST AND FOUND

Ida May didn't see the boy at first. Instead she felt his presence in the same way that she sometimes felt that her own son, dead now twenty years, was in the kitchen with her, inhabiting the fuzzy spots in her mind, making the room feel a little less chilly. She likened the feeling to those rare moments in church when, during her favorite hymn, she could shut her eyes and not worry about anything, even the fact that she, unlike her husband, no longer believed in the god she was pretending to worship.

Usually these moments lasted only a second or two, but on the morning the boy showed up the feeling stayed with her as she cracked eggs for her husband's breakfast and brewed two pots of coffee so that her sisters would have some while they helped her bake pies for the church bake sale. Ida May didn't notice the boy until she had scrambled the eggs and brewed the first pot of coffee. Then, as she was taking down mugs from the cupboard, she saw him: a boy sitting at the window seat her husband had built years ago. She didn't make eye contact with him or even pause as she opened the cupboard door and took out two mugs. It was as though she had seen a crack in the wall or a stain on the counter, something which required her attention but not before other pressing matters like getting her husband's breakfast out to the dining room. So all she did was sigh, pour the coffee, and wipe her hands on her apron. Later, once her two sisters arrived, they asked her how she could be so calm about the situation. Weren't you worried that Franklin would come in and see him? At this Ida May laughed, smoothed down her apron, and said, "When was the last time you saw Franklin go near the kitchen?"

Her sisters both laughed, but the good feeling only lasted a moment before there were other questions, all of them asked by Maggie, her older sister. What's his name? Where did he come from? Who are his parents? How did he get inside your house? Maggie asked these questions one after another and with such force Ida May felt the need to sit down for the first time since she had woken up. The heat from the kitchen and the fact she hadn't eaten anything yet made her feel lightheaded. It seemed like the old adage "If you can't stand the heat ..." applied here, and it made her feel ridiculous and childlike.

"I need a biscuit or something," Ida May said.

Allie, the youngest of the sisters, put before her a plate with a biscuit and some apple slices that hadn't made it into any of the pies. She refilled her coffee, too, and told Maggie to give her a minute. Ida May thanked her and then ate the biscuit slowly, thinking about her sister's questions and her overall belief that truth was attainable if you just applied yourself. It reminded her of how Franklin had acted with the doctors when their son had died. He had been just as upset as her, but he took it out on the people around him, demanding answers from the doctors about why their son had died in the night. She hadn't even listened to their responses because the only truth in the situation was that their boy was gone and she would always feel responsible, regardless of what they said.

After taking the last bite of her biscuit, Ida May wiped some crumbs from her mouth and stood up.

"He doesn't speak English."

This was basically a lie, an assumption she had made based on the color of the boy's skin. In reality, Ida May hadn't tried to speak to the boy even once. After serving Franklin his breakfast, she had returned to the kitchen and fixed a plate of eggs for the boy. She had set the plate directly in the boy's hands but didn't say a word. There was a moment during the exchange where they both opened their mouths, but it never went any further than a loud breath and a shared glance which seemed to suggest an apology for almost interrupting each other.

Maggie walked over to the window seat and tapped the boy on the shoulder. The boy appeared to be looking at something in the distance, perhaps the orchard or even the country road which lay beyond. He didn't turn around until Maggie tapped him again.

"Do you understand me?" Maggie said. "Can you speak English?"

The boy looked up at her but said nothing. Maggie continued asking questions, mostly the same ones she had raised earlier, and her voice seemed to get louder with each one so that by the time she was finished it bordered on yelling. She had her hands on her hips, too, head bent forward some, as if she needed to get even closer for her words to take effect. To someone passing by the window she would've looked like an angry mom — or based on Maggie's age, perhaps a grandmother — scolding her child. The boy listened to a few of the questions but turned his head back toward the window before she was finished, a move which seemed to increase the volume of Maggie's voice.

Ida May watched this happen from across the room, her hands squeezed into tight fists, fingernails digging into the skin of her palms.

"Stop it, Maggie," Ida May said. "He doesn't understand."

Maggie stopped yelling at the boy and crossed the room until she was standing right in front of Ida May.

"You're losing your mind, Ida" she said. "There's no way this situation can turn out well."

"So was I supposed to just kick him out of my house or something?" Ida May said. "That doesn't sound very Christian to me."

Allie laughed. The noise didn't last long before it cut out. Even when Maggie swung her head around it was like it had never happened. Allie looked as pious as if she was taking in a Sunday sermon. Ida May felt proud of what she had said, although she noticed that she had unconsciously taken a couple steps back, enough to where Maggie couldn't slap or push her, both of which she had experienced when they were kids and she had done something her sister hadn't liked. After realizing that she had stepped backwards, Ida May held her head up and looked her sister in the eye. The look on Maggie's face reminded Ida of their mother, which immediately made her think of the old woman's last days in the nursing home, the days when she didn't recognize any of her daughters. Ida looked away from her sister and over to the apple slices on her plate. Already they were rotting in several places.

"I'm sorry," Ida said. "I didn't know what else to do."

Maggie bit down on her lower lip, crossed her arms, and said, "Well, he's our problem now."

Sometime later in the morning, when most of the pies were either cooling or in the oven, Allie tried speaking to the boy. She spoke to him using the little Spanish she knew, words she had picked up from the man she was dating. What struck Ida May was that Allie was talking slowly, the foreign words coming out slower than she had ever heard this language spoken. If the boy understood any of her words, he didn't show it. He was looking right at her, but his expression never changed. For long stretches of time he wouldn't even blink.

Ida May watched the boy closely, taking note of his appearance in ways she hadn't earlier. His eyes, for instance, she found to be an unusual mix of brown with flecks of green and gold. For some reason the phrase "gypsy eyes" came to mind. She also noticed that his haircut was of the same basic type that she, along with many other women she knew, gave to her kids when they were young so they could save money. Rather than focusing on style, the haircut focused mainly on keeping the hair from flipping over the ear or hanging over the eyes.

In general the boy was cute, but not just in the way that all kids were more or less cute. Ida May could tell by his face that he would someday be the type of man women would call handsome. Even before Allie finished talking to him, Ida May felt a certain attachment to him. She told herself that it was mainly because of the boy's situation; whatever had led him to sneak into her kitchen must've been bad. If it had just been her and Allie in the kitchen, Ida May would've picked the boy up already, held him to her chest, felt his breath on her neck, ran her hand through his hair. Since she couldn't do this, she did something else which came natural to her. She waited until Allie gave up trying to talk to the boy and then cut a slice of pie from one that was cooling on the windowsill. Ida May could feel Maggie watching her, judging her both for her weakness toward the child and her laziness; since getting the kitchen ready, she had done little in the way of pie making, a point she justified by telling herself that the boy needed her attention. But even she would admit she was taking this to the extreme by standing near the window seat and watching him eat. After finishing the pie, the boy nodded to her and Allie, stood up, and took his plate over to the sink.

"He's so polite," Ida May said. "He did the same thing earlier with the plate of eggs I fixed him."

"Maggie does have a point," Allie said. "I'm not sure what we can do for him if he won't talk."

Ida May filled the sink with hot water and soap and started scrubbing the dishes from breakfast. The water nearly scalded her hand, but she didn't bother adjusting the tap again to make it colder. This was how she had washed dishes since her son had died. Although she was no longer religious, she still liked the idea of penance, only she believed it was better if you felt some physical pain, too.

"Did you hear me, Ida?" Allie said.

Ida May nodded.

"Just let me finish these dishes," she said. "And then we'll figure it out."

They discussed the issue over more coffee and slices of the pie which Ida had given to the boy. Their conversation was hurried because Franklin would be home for lunch soon.

"I think we should take him to the police," Maggie said. "Let them sort it out."

"We can't do that," Ida May said.

Allie nodded.

"They'll probably send him back to Mexico," she said. "Especially after what happened at The Tap."

Even though Ida May didn't keep up on what happened in town much anymore, she still knew about the migrant worker who had stabbed a trucker over a game of pool. The backlash against illegal immigrants had led to rallies, protests, and other assorted meetings. People in favor of changing the law held their own events while those who took a more moderate stance, like Franklin, worried there would be more violence.

"Why would that be such a bad thing?" Maggie said.

At these words Ida May immediately looked over at the boy. If he understood what had just been said, his face didn't show it. He was looking out the window again.

Allie shook her head and looked down at the crumbs of pie on her plate as if she were considering another slice. Without looking up, Allie asked Maggie if that was how she felt about all Mexicans.

"Only the ones here illegally."

Allie pushed her plate aside and leaned both elbows on the table.

"What do you think would happen to the town if all the immigrants suddenly disappeared?"

Maggie started to answer, but Ida May cut her off.

"We need to get him downstairs," she said. "I hear Franklin's truck pulling in."

Maggie didn't stay for lunch or even finish cleaning up the kitchen. She left when Franklin sat down on the sofa and started telling them about the migrant workers that had died in a car crash he passed by on his way to work.

"All of them were already dead by the time I passed the scene," he said. "The police were only just starting to clean it up."

Franklin went on to say how bad the scene had been, but each time he tried to find words for it he stopped, pressed his lips together, and shook his head. Finally he told them it was the worst thing he'd ever seen. Ida May went to his side at the same moment Maggie headed for the front door. She left and slammed the door without saying goodbye.

From across the room the two sisters looked at each other with their hands clasped and eyes raised. It was the same look they'd shared a few minutes earlier when they'd led the boy downstairs. Maggie had just told them both that she wouldn't be held responsible for what happened if they got in trouble. The way she hung on to the word *if* and shook her head made it seem like she really meant *when*. And the gestures her prediction brought out were like a tell in poker, something neither sister could help doing. Ida May expected her husband to notice and then ask why Maggie had left so suddenly, but he just sat there shaking his head.

"It was bad, Ida," he said. "Really bad."

Ida May leaned over so she could hold his hand. His skin felt dry and warm.

"I'll fix us all lunch and then clean up," Allie said.

Franklin stopped shaking his head and turned toward Allie.

"Thank you," he said. "But I don't feel much like eating right now."

Ida May and Allie went downstairs right after Franklin went back to work. They headed past the canning shelves that would get filled up soon with crabapple jelly, apples, and peaches. They walked past the workbench where Franklin used to sit with their boys and build little cars made out of pine. And finally they came to a corner piled with boxes containing all the clothes and toys that had belonged to Mitchell. For some reason Ida had told the boy to wait there, only now he was gone.

Without saying a word, Ida left and searched the rest of the basement. She looked in the furnace room and then under the stairs before she returned to the corner.

"I don't understand," she said. "We brought him down here less than an hour ago."

She started to look around again, but Allie grabbed her arm before she could get anywhere.

"He's gone, Ida."

Something about the familiarity of the words and the pressure of fingertips squeezing her arm made Ida twist away.

"Maybe he went upstairs or out in the backyard," Ida said. "He couldn't have gone far."

Allie stood so that she was face to face with Ida, blocking Ida's path to the rest of the basement.

"I hate to say it, Ida, but I think it's for the best that we don't have to deal with this."

Allie took her hand and motioned for them to sit down on one of the boxes. They sat there quietly for some time. Ida looked from one box to another, going through the contents in her head. If she had been alone, she would have opened up each one, holding shirts close to her chest and running her fingers over the material as if they were rosary beads. This was an activity she normally reserved for his birthday, and, in addition to the overwhelming sadness it brought out, she also felt guilty because she had let Franklin convert Mitchell's bedroom into a sewing room, which meant all their boy's stuff got shoved into boxes.

Since the room had been finished, though, she hadn't sewn or mended a single garment, which had ended up costing their family more on clothing. At first she had been mad at her husband even though she knew it didn't make sense to keep Mitchell's room the same when he was gone. What made her so upset was that either way the decision seemed final.

"Did you want to be alone?" Allie said.

Ida lifted her head with a sudden awareness that she'd been staring at the concrete floor. She then stood up, brushed off the dust from her dress, and shook her head.

"We should finish up the pies," Ida said.

In reality there wasn't much to do besides covering them and boxing them up for the sale, but Ida needed some reason to get them out of the basement. As they reached the top of the stairs, the light from the kitchen and the blue autumn sky were blinding. Both sisters shielded their faces as they walked to the table.

"I didn't want to ask this," Ida said. "But do you think Carlos could help us look for the boy?"

Allie took her hands off the pie she was about to wrap up and smoothed them down her pants.

"You know he has enough trouble with people in town without getting involved in something like this."

Ida knew her sister was right. People in town assumed Carlos was an illegal because the majority of people with his skin color were. Still, it seemed like he would be interested in helping out others who weren't as well off.

"I'm sorry," Ida said. "But I felt like I had to ask."

Allie stepped away from the table and started to leave the kitchen. Before she left the room she turned around and said, "Would you have asked Franklin?"

After finishing up with the pies, Ida still had a while before her husband came home. She sat in the window seat, looking out on the road and the orchard. At any moment she expected to see the sheriff's car approach. She didn't think she could get into any trouble, but the thought of explaining what had happened to anyone didn't sit well. Probably she could have phoned Maggie to see if she had followed through on her threat of getting the authorities involved, but Ida didn't want to give Maggie the satisfaction of knowing she had upset her. It seemed like her only other choices were to go out looking for the boy or else continue sitting where she was until it was time to make supper.

Leaving the house had some appeal since it meant she'd be doing something, although Ida knew she didn't have the courage to actually go to the places where the boy might have gone.

And even if she found him, then what? Adopting a young child didn't make sense at her age. Plus, this wouldn't be a real possibility for her or even for Allie given the current atmosphere in town. Really, all she wanted was a little more time with the boy, just the two of them. She tried to tell herself the reason was that they had both been through something horrible and this gave them an understanding. If she had been totally sure this was true, she would've gone to look for him rather than get up from the window seat and start dinner.

At the table, neither she nor Franklin ate very much. They didn't speak much either, not until he set down his silverware and apologized for not having much appetite.

"I still keep thinking about that crash," he said. "A fellow at work told me most of them had kids."

Ida didn't look up from her plate.

"No one's sure where they are now. I guess folks are out there looking for them, but there's a lot of ground to cover, especially in the orchards."

Ida looked at her husband from across the table then out the window. The sky was nearing dark now, only a yellowish smudge remained on the horizon. Franklin pushed his plate forward.

"I was thinking I'd help out with the search," he said.

She stood up and started clearing. When she got to his place she set her hand on his shoulder. He craned his neck some to look at her. It seemed like the time to explain how the boy showed up and left just as suddenly. And perhaps this confession would bring up other feelings she had held back over the years. The weight of it all was something she wanted to be rid of, but it had become a part of her, too.

"What do you think of that idea?"

She almost said that it didn't matter, that the kids would have a rough life no matter what people in town did for them. But instead she told him to go.

"You sure, Ida?"

She nodded. Within minutes he was gone, leaving her alone with the dishes and the hot water in the sink. She stood there looking outside even though it was full dark now and there wasn't much to see. Soon Franklin would gather at the church with the other men, and then all of them would head to the orchards and fields. Ida May liked the idea of her husband out there with the other men, searching by flashlight. She liked the notion of a child bringing people together instead of pulling them apart.

OUR CASTLE

No one had expected the mansion known as Woodrow Castle to ever sell, especially to someone who planned on using it as their primary residence. Once, during the early nineties, a group of venture capitalists backed a young couple's attempt to run it as a bed and breakfast, but it didn't last even a year; evidently the couple didn't accurately factor in the cost of heating such a massive building. Although the mansion was in superb shape structurally, the expense of such a place, not to mention the overt and aristocratic show of wealth, didn't make sense in our Midwestern town, a city still trying to recover from the failing auto industry. Essentially, we viewed Woodrow Castle as an anachronism, albeit one so grand it would maybe never get torn down. While we all held this practical view, we had always been secretly glad no one owned the place.

Jealousy had everything to do with this sentiment. Every time one of us drove or walked by the place we would fantasize about what we do if it were ours, the parties we'd have, the artwork we'd display on the walls, the books we'd buy to fill what were surely massive shelves lining the walls of the study. No one in the neighborhood made enough to afford such a grand house, but we all worked hard at our jobs, just as hard, if not harder, as anyone who actually could afford the place. The main difference between us and people who could buy was that we did not come from money.

For this reason, when the house was bought, we expected it to have been one of the old money names connected with the pharmaceutical company in town, someone trying to strengthen their empire by establishing a more visible display of their wealth. But when we found out it was Monroe, we were shocked, mainly because he was the owner of the largest residential building company in the area, a company that churned out new houses that, although large, were nearly devoid of personality or character; for him to own the most unique house in town, a building that took a total of two years to plan and build as opposed to a month, seemed at odds with his sensibilities.

But, the energetic drive behind his company's rapid success was evident as soon as he took possession of Woodrow Castle. Within days there were signs of life: we saw women busy cleaning the windows and sweeping off the wraparound porch; we saw men stooped over the grapevines in the vineyards; we saw barrel chested men unloading three separate moving vans. Despite all this activity, we didn't catch sight of the man himself until he threw his first party.

We had received invitations by mail a few weeks after he moved in telling us there would be a cocktail party Friday evening. Besides the time, the only other piece of information on the card was a line saying that formal attire was expected. We showed up dressed as instructed, expecting perhaps to be greeted by a butler, some stately old gentlemen who would direct us to where the party was being held. Instead, a man in his late thirties dressed in a gray pinstripe suit met us at the door. He stuck out his hand to each of us and said, "I'm J.A. Monroe. Nice to meet all of you. Go ahead on up to the ballroom on the third floor. I'll be up in a minute." Before we could respond, he moved off down a hallway. It took a moment for us to follow his instructions, because we were all a little stunned by his appearance, which didn't match up in any way with our expectations of what this man should look like. Monroe, with his slick designer suit and black wavy hair, looked more like a rock star or actor, rather than a business executive.

After regaining our composure, we climbed the stairs to the third floor. On our way we could hear the sound of musicians warming up: bass runs, scales played on trumpets and saxophones, jazz chords on piano and guitar, drum fills. The staircase spit us out into a long hallway, with two doors on each side. The remainder of the floor was taken up by the ballroom. Upon entering, we saw the band platform and the six musicians we had heard, as well as a full wet bar on the far wall, complete with a bartender. All of this, combined with the overall ambience, made us feel like we had stepped into the life we were meant to live.

After getting our first drink, we stood around and waited. Before long the band started playing, but no one stepped onto the floor immediately. It was as though we were waiting for Monroe to show up and officially begin the party. However, other people began filtering into the ballroom: men and women a few years our junior who hit the floor without bothering to have their first cocktail. Their style of dress was similar to Monroe's: modern, fashionable, a little bit edgy. Although we considered ourselves to possess these same qualities, by comparison we looked conservative and out of date. Certainly this played a part in how long it took us to join them on the floor: most of us had at least one more cocktail before joining them.

The band had started off playing slow jazz, music we could move to without much exertion, but after a couple numbers they switched to swing, and we had no choice but to adapt, even though most of us had little experience in this area. The newcomers would switch dance partners frequently, at first rotating amongst themselves but then extending this practice to us. They would reach for a hand with such confidence, even those of us who preferred to only dance with our spouses couldn't turn down.

Our new partners showed us moves and steps we were unfamiliar with. This could've been interpreted as showing off or being condescending, but there was a playfulness in their smiles that we took as a challenge. You want to keep up with us, right? And perhaps the way some of them touched someone's back or hips or held their hand was a bit too suggestive, but in the spirit of the night we went with it, hoping our spouse didn't notice or making sure our own behavior didn't cross into similar territory.

For most of us, this wasn't too difficult; however, as the evening continued and the drinking and dancing grew more frenzied, inhibitions disappeared. The first one to transgress was Hayden Briggs. The way he told the story it wasn't exactly his fault, though. He had left the ballroom to find the bathroom when a woman pulled him into one of the rooms adjoining the hallway. The room was completely dark, and, before he could say a word, the woman had her hands on him and her mouth pressed to his. According to Hayden, he had thought the woman was his wife, because the two of them had been dancing passionately all evening (except for the occasional dance with one of the strangers), and he had already thought the chances of them being intimate that night were good. But after a while, Hayden realized that the woman was not his wife or, for that matter, anyone he knew. What made him come to this realization is something he never would say, although we guessed Hayden must've learned the truth by touching her breasts or butt and not feeling the shape he was used to.

Certainly what happened to Hayden that night could've happened to anyone, but the situation went beyond a mistake when he stayed in the room for several minutes after realizing the woman wasn't his wife. When he told us the story, it was with equal parts guilt and excitement that those few minutes with the mysterious woman were the most dangerous and erotic he'd ever experienced, and yet he didn't take the situation to its logical conclusion: when the woman guided his hand up her dress and down her panties, he pulled away. Then he quickly straightened his clothes, left the room, and went to the bar for a drink. It wasn't until the cocktail glass reached his lips that he smelled his fingers and realized his hand had lingered for longer than he'd realized.

For the next several days, we thought about the party a great deal, recalling the evening in scattered fragments, like trying to piece together a half-remembered dream. No one could remember how long they had stayed or how many drinks they had consumed or how many people they had danced with. The confusion bothered us some, but there was also something ecstatic and reckless about our behavior that we reveled in, for certainly this was not like us. We were all solid, respectable citizens, lawyers and doctors, business owners and managers. We didn't stay out all night, worrying the babysitters. We didn't lose track of how many drinks we had had. In fact, weren't we always critical of people like that? Didn't we criticize their behavior as being low class? But none of us could deny the pleasure we had felt that night.

When we spoke of it with each other, we realized that no one had really seen Monroe. A couple people claimed to have caught a glimpse of him on the dance floor or at the bar, but admittedly these sightings were not without reservations: they were glimpses at best, and they occurred later in the evening, after guests stopped keeping track of their alcohol consumption. Thus, the possibility was brought up that he had left his own party early on, perhaps on business. This theory seemed bizarre, but over the next couple weeks we never saw Monroe, not even a glimpse of him pulling into his driveway, so the possibility of him being on a business trip seemed realistic.

An even more extreme theory was that he had merely rented Woodrow Castle for one night. Although this seemed unlikely, the fact that we hadn't seen any signs of occupancy since that night did give this notion some weight. Then, once most of us (most likely with the exception of Hayden) had stopped thinking about Monroe and the party, we received another invitation. This invitation was slicker than the first: it was printed on glossy black cardstock with silver lettering, and on the bottom corner was a picture of a mansion, as well as the words Woodrow Castle. It almost looked like something put out by a business rather than an individual.

We all immediately cleared any plans we had for the coming Friday, although Hayden did so with reluctance and guilt. When we showed up at the door, Monroe was there to greet us again. This time, however, he walked us up to the ballroom himself. Along the way he pointed to various features of the mansion, describing them in great detail like he was a tour guide or the curator of a museum. He spoke reverently of the woodwork, its age and the type of woods used. He gestured toward windows with lead mullions or stained glass. He made us pause before a massive built-in cabinet. Monroe frequently positioned himself out of the light so that we focused on the detail rather on the man talking about it. His voice, though, did seem odd: he spoke with passion, but the depth of his tone suggested someone older.

At the time we didn't think much of these details or of his behavior; all we wanted was to get the evening started. Later, though, we remembered what Monroe did for a living and thought it strange. How could someone that seemed to favor unique detail build houses that, more often than not, looked exactly the same? However, once we arrived at the ballroom, our thoughts were focused purely on the evening ahead of us.

Monroe told us to enjoy ourselves, and then he walked back downstairs, presumably to wait for the other guests. The same jazz band was there. This time they had already warmed up and were playing, urging us onto the dance floor with melodies that were a haunting mix of familiarity and deft improvisation. Before long, the other guests showed up. We looked for some of the familiar faces from the time before, the people we had danced with like lovers, but none of them were here (those of us who had heard about Hayden's encounter cautiously looked over at him and saw a look of relief). Instead, a new crowd of people emerged from the staircase and started dancing.

All of them were just as beautiful and sophisticated as the people we had seen before. Looking back, we like to think that if the same crowd had shown up, the thrill we got from dancing with them, from sharing such public, yet private, intimate moments wouldn't have existed. However, our excitement was the same, if not greater, than the last time. And by the time the evening was half over, most of us were drunk more on the presence of the strangers than the expensive booze we were being served.

Around ten o'clock, just as the party seemed to be at its peak, Kelly Sanders entered a room off the hallway and had sex with a man she thought was her husband. She claimed that, while dancing with her husband, she had whispered for him to meet her in one of the rooms. Although she clung to this story until the end, even when her husband found out the truth, a variety of evidence suggested she had known what she was doing. To begin with, all of us saw her dance only once with her husband, and it was toward the beginning of the night, a good couple of hours before the actual deed. Plus, we saw Kelly on the dance floor with the same partner, one of the new guests, quite a few times.

Even if her story was to be believed, wouldn't she have realized some difference between this stranger and her husband? The likelihood of these two men having the same physical features in every way was low, and certainly there were other differences in the way people made love that would've made her realize she was having an affair.

Although we were skeptical, to say the least, of her story, there wasn't a person among us that didn't secretly imagine themselves in her position, fantasizing about the guilty, yet intense passion she must've felt. Oh, it was wrong, we knew that, but something about the grandeur of the mansion and the way it recalled another century made everything that happened at the parties seem removed from everyday life. In those rare moments we allowed ourselves to consider the impact these affairs would have on people's lives; we quieted the guilt by telling ourselves that neither Hayden nor Kelly were happy in their marriages, otherwise why would they have been unfaithful?

The next invitation arrived within days. Now that we knew what to expect, or at least thought we did, all we could think about was the party. At work, we were distracted easily, and irritated by the seemingly mundane tasks and questions our jobs required. When we arrived at the party, we threw ourselves into the pleasures it had to offer as if we had been prisoners our whole lives: we immediately had several drinks as we eyed the strange yet beautiful men and women filling up the room.

Unlike the other nights, we saw Monroe frequently. He danced with every woman in the room. He drank cocktails with the men, holding court at the bar, telling jokes and stories with an ease that suggested he was either born with these gifts or he had carefully cultivated them over the years.

While this was going on, at least a few of us got lost in the revelry and forgot the vows we had made to our spouses. Leila Briggs was among those who were unfaithful that night. When asked why, she grew agitated. One of her eyes twitched, and she couldn't sit still. Finally, after several minutes had gone by, she said, I don't know, her words staccato clips of anger and confusion. Others in her situation had basically the same response. Their behavior was curious, to be sure, especially since it differed so much from Hayden and Kelly's accounts. All sorts of theories were put forth to explain what had happened. Some suggested that the guilty had been drugged and, as a result, could not fully remember (and were not responsible for) their actions. Another theory was that the infidelities were revenge based.

While this possibility had some merit, especially as it related to Leila, there were flaws, too. To begin with, there is some doubt as to whether Leila had known about Hayden's encounter at that point. Then there was the matter of the others. Had their spouses already been unfaithful? Had they danced too much or too close with one of the guests at the party? Because there were too many unknowns attached to this theory, we tended to discount it. Perhaps the strongest idea was that they simply had felt compelled to cheat. And perhaps whatever factors led to this decision were currently beyond their understanding, which would explain their bewildered responses.

Whatever the reason or reasons were, a number of us had changed our attitudes about Monroe's parties. Although we had enjoyed ourselves more than any recent memory could recall, we felt that some line had been crossed. The evidence to support this view was certainly growing, but only a small number actually felt this way. Initially, those of us with this mindset decided we would not attend the next party. However, once the date of the next one grew close, we changed our minds, telling ourselves and others that we would go to protect others from making mistakes they would surely one day regret. We would not drink. We would not dance. We wouldn't mingle with the guests. Essentially, we would be chaperones, those sentry-like figures at the edge of the dance floor like we remembered from the homecomings and proms of our youth.

At first, we stuck to our plan. But, as the night progressed, we grew weary of standing on the sidelines, especially when we were used to being a part of the action. So, gradually we slipped onto the dance floor or headed to the bar. Those first dances and drinks were almost as intense as what we had felt the first night, both because we had gone without for longer and because we felt an odd mix of exhilaration and guilt for leaving our posts.

Strangely, those of us who had chosen to act as chaperones were also the same ones guilty of betrayal that night. By the end of the night we all had ended up in the quiet darkness of various rooms in the mansion with men and women whose names we didn't even know. Yet, when it came time to perform the actual act, none of us were able. Instead, we apologized profusely and then slumped to the ground, where we lay half naked, confessing our most hidden secrets, memories and events we hadn't even told our own spouses, events we had tried so hard to bury, to the point that some of us didn't fully believe they had happened. The release we felt upon doing so was exhausting, all consuming, more powerful than any orgasm we could've experienced. Afterwards, we allowed whoever we were with to hold us briefly, and then, in silence, we dressed and left the room.

Although we discussed with one another the general nature of what happened that night, none of us would ever repeat the exact secrets, no matter how hard our spouses or friends pressed us. And the curious thing was that we had no logical reason to not repeat the disclosure. If we had done it once, wouldn't it be easier to do a second time? One theory that circulated was that, once unburdened from the weight of the secret, it was if the event, no matter how horrible or embarrassing, did not belong to us any longer.

When word of our experiences began to circulate, our craving for the parties reached new heights. Everyone wanted in on this quasi-religious confession. All of us, it seemed, had some dark truth nestled in the hollows of our consciousness. Some of us questioned why these secrets couldn't just be confessed through more normal channels: priests, rabbis, psychologists, and the like. Perhaps because some of our secrets were too sordid to mention in a house of God or even to a respected (and highly paid) professional. Or perhaps there was something of the erotic mixed in with the confession. Still others said that the nakedness had more to do with being born again than sex.

For better or worse, though, no one else had the chance to take part in this ritual. We waited for the customary invitation to be sent out, but nothing came. One week went by, then two weeks, and during this time we saw no activity in or around the mansion. We made sure to drive by the house at various times of the day and night, but still we saw nothing. After a month passed, Joseph Sanders, who was currently trying to decide whether or not he should divorce his wife, snuck across the lawn of Woodrow Castle one night so he could peer inside. Although we certainly couldn't openly condone his actions, we all were eager to find out what he had seen. It was empty, he told us. The entire place cleared out; it was like no one had ever lived there at all.

At first, no one believed his account. How could such a massive home get vacated without us having any idea? And, even if Monroe really was leaving, wouldn't there be a for sale sign in front of the house? Whatever the explanation, the fact remained that there was no evidence to refute Sanders's report. The problem was that none of us were ready to move on. The tradition of the weekly cocktail party already figured so heavily into our daily thoughts and lives that it was difficult to imagine life without it. We had looked forward to the events so much and built up their importance far beyond what is reasonable that now our lives seemed to lack purpose.

Given enough time, though, we surely would've moved on with our lives. However, not even a week after Sanders had given us his findings, reports began to surface of men in suits and women in dresses standing upon the balcony adjoining the ballroom, the site of most of the cocktail parties. These sightings came from people that didn't live in our neighborhood, so they carried more weight than if we had seen them ourselves.

Our first reaction was disbelief. How could people be living there, much less having a party, after we had confirmed that the place was empty? But, as more and more people claimed to have seen the same thing, our disbelief turned into anger. If Monroe still occupied the house and was throwing parties, why had he not invited us? What had we done? We felt as though we had been cast out of the Garden of Eden.

We weren't sure exactly how to proceed with this new knowledge, but we were determined to see the parties with our own eyes. So we anxiously waited until the next Friday and then proceeded to observe the mansion. It was decided that only a few of us, chosen for our reliable nature, would go. We waited until about an hour after the parties usually got started and then walked over there. Truthfully, we didn't have much of a unified plan if there was in fact a party going on. Some of us merely wanted to observe, while others wanted to actually go inside.

As we approached, we didn't hear any noises that suggested there was a party. But, even from a distance, we could see people on the third story balcony. However, the closer we got, the more something seemed off: no one was moving. The moment we realized this we stopped walking to get a better look. We waited at least ten minutes and still there was no movement. Someone suggested that maybe they were playing some sort of game with us, mocking us outcasts. Then, as the minutes stretched on with no change, someone said, "They must be mannequins." This thought hadn't yet occurred to us, but once it had been mentioned, the idea made sense. Even before we got close enough to confirm this theory, it took on a sense of irrefutable truth.

To verify our theory, we stood at the edge of the lawn at Woodrow Castle while one of us looked up at the balcony through binoculars. He only had the binoculars up for a moment before taking them away from his eyes, stuffing them into a bag of supplies (which also included a camera in case we needed to document anything we saw) and shaking his head. The rest of us asked the same question: why?

We pondered this as we trudged back to our respective homes. It was a beautiful night, one of the first warm nights in spring where the redbuds and magnolias were in bloom, but we took no notice. Instead, we discussed possible theories that would explain the presence of the mannequins. The most popular notion was that someone, probably Monroe, was taunting us. This also led some of us to think that Monroe was some sort of voyeur and that perhaps he had been in some of the rooms as we cheated on our spouses or laid bare our most private thoughts. Perhaps he had recorded them, too.

But, based on the lack of activity at the mansion, it seemed more likely that this was a prank, maybe one orchestrated by someone in our neighborhood, perhaps one of us who had not committed any serious transgression at the parties. Another theory that was proposed said that the mannequins functioned as an invitation. The few that supported this notion wanted us to return home, call up the others in the neighborhood, quickly find sitters for those of us with children, and return to the mansion dressed in our best suits and dresses. Although this idea seemed ridiculous in most ways, its supporters did raise one solid point: Hadn't the invitations changed once before? They argued that the mannequins were yet another shift in the way Monroe got the word out. Maybe he wanted fewer people to attend, only those people who cared enough to see if anyone still lived in Woodrow Castle.

However, when we returned home and called everyone else in the neighborhood, the consensus was that it was merely a prank. Considering everything that had happened, we probably held this view to protect ourselves from possible disappointment. After all, most of us had again tried to get on with our normal routines, plunging

ourselves into our jobs with a feverish intensity, almost like
we were trying to make up for the months of partial
distraction. Still, there were moments when thoughts of the
mansion would creep in: the memories of a hand on the hip
of some stranger's body, the inscrutable faces of the jazz
band, the cool burn of the first cocktail of the evening.
Some of us who were particularly gifted at keeping these
thoughts out during the day claimed to pay for it with
haunting dreams they could only escape by taking sleeping
pills. More than one of our bosses noticed a change in our
performance at work. Our children kept us at a distance,
often withholding the affection they had so freely given. We
weren't sure what scared us more, the fact that we weren't
the same people anymore, or the fact that we wouldn't care
about this change if it meant being able to return to the
mansion.

The mannequins were out again the next Friday. No
one had seen them all week, nor had we seen any signs of
life at the mansion, but Friday evening they were back, and
the staging had changed significantly. Before the
mannequins had just looked like normal men and women at
a party, but now they were arranged provocatively, pants
lowered to ankles, pelvises thrust together. And while the
lower halves were posed in an obviously lewd fashion, from
the waist up they were meant to look like they were simply
enjoying the party: they held cocktail glasses, and their
smiles suggested someone in the group had just told a joke.

The combined effect was more than a bit disturbing.
If the mannequins were meant to be a joke, the person or
persons behind it had gone too far. It was a slap in the face
for us to be reminded of what we couldn't have anymore,
but it was far worse to have our behavior mocked and put
on public display. People from other neighborhoods could
see what we had done. True, they might not fully
understand the full implications; however, the thought of
any scrutiny made us uneasy. We knew we had to deal with

the situation before we lost any more sleep, but the question was how?

Someone suggested going to the police, but this idea was quickly shot down. Whoever had staged the mannequins had committed no crime, unless they were not the owners, in which case they would've been trespassing. Another suggestion was to just let things blow over. It's probably just some teenagers playing a prank. We gave this a moment's discussion but quickly discarded it as too involved for a bunch of kids, which meant there was probably something sinister behind the acts. At this point, the amount of support for the theory of Monroe being the person responsible grew, so much so that we designated someone to go to Monroe's office and make contact. We didn't have a solid plan of what should be said to him, but the idea of having any plan at all appealed to us.

So on Tuesday, Nolan Patterson, chosen because he was perhaps the least memorable among us, went downtown to the office of the Monroe Group. He had called the day before, explaining to the secretary that he was interested in having a new home built but would like to speak directly to the owner first. He was surprised when the secretary told him the appointment would be the very next day. At the appointed time, the secretary ushered Nolan in to a spacious office bright with sunlight from a window wall behind Monroe's desk. A middle aged man wearing an ill fitting navy blue suit stood up from his desk and shook hands with Nolan. Even before the handshake was over, Nolan said, "There must be some mistake. I made an appointment with J.A. Monroe."

The man, still gripping Nolan's hand, smiled and said, "That's who you're looking at."

Those of us present to hear Nolan tell the story could imagine how his face must've turned white or his heart skipped a beat and his mind raced, trying to make some kind of meaning out of this revelation. Luckily, he had

had the presence of mind to carry on with the meeting instead of rushing out the door. After regaining his composure, he pretended that he was there to start planning the design of his new house. Toward the end of the meeting, he had the quick wit to ask Monroe if perhaps he had any sons or close male relatives living in town.

"Nope," Monroe had said. "I have plenty of female cousins and no kids, so I guess that makes me the last in the line."

We didn't know what to make of this information Nolan had delivered to us. The possibility that he had made some kind of mistake seemed unlikely, so the main questions centered around the identity of the man who had called himself Monroe. If he wasn't some kind of con man or criminal, then why had he not used his real name? There was also the question of how he had acquired possession of the mansion. Purchasing the house and then abandoning it less than two months later seemed unlikely. Someone suggested the possibility that he had rented Woodrow Castle to host several parties, the purpose of which was to get us to compromise ourselves in various ways. Supporters of this theory believed that we would soon be receiving blackmail letters. Although there was a lot of evidence backing up this idea, the fact that no letters had arrived did cast some doubt. Moreover, the cost of renting the mansion, even for only a couple months, would've been so high that the individual would've needed a quick return on his investment.

Another theory, perhaps not as fully fleshed out, was that the person calling himself Monroe had neither bought the mansion nor rented it. Instead, he had observed how the mansion had been unoccupied for a long time and simply walked in and started pretending it was his. The idea that Woodrow Castle had been there to use all this time we'd lived in the neighborhood seemed absurd, but the more we thought about it, the more it made sense. If the mansion was owned by a bank or investment group, then only on rare occasions would anyone come out to check in on the mansion's status. Perhaps the man posing as Monroe even worked for the bank or was part of the investment group. Whatever the case was, if this theory was true, then someone had committed a crime, which meant that we'd at least have grounds to go to the police if necessary.

At that point, we did something we should've done much earlier: check with the city to see who owned the mansion. We trusted Nolan Patterson with this important task, which he accepted only after we insisted it would be the last time we called upon him. Later that same day he came back to tell us what he'd found. Apparently Woodrow Castle had only changed hands twice: once when the mansion was sold by the heirs of Joseph Woodrow to the venture capitalists, and then once more when the city bought it. The city is planning on turning it into a historical museum but hasn't raised the money yet, Nolan explained.

Although this wasn't the answer we wanted, it did give us an angle to pursue. All we had to do was check out people who worked for the city, especially higher-up officials, and we would find the person we were looking for. True, this would take considerably more time than other options, but it would at least keep our minds occupied.

However, before we could even get much research done, the mannequins showed up again, and the staging was even more insulting. A growing number of people in the neighborhood wanted to hand the matter over to the police and be done with it. Of course, most of this group had not transgressed as severely at the parties so they didn't have as much to lose, but it was getting harder to ignore the situation. This group informed the rest of us that if we didn't handle the matter ourselves by the end of the night that they would turn it over to the authorities.

It was with this fear in mind that we decided to knock on the door of Woodrow Castle. When we arrived there, we were immediately struck by the sight of the mannequins: mannequins on the lawn, mannequins on the balcony, mannequins on the porch; all of them naked at the waist and positioned on their knees. The entire effect was like a cheap zombie movie, where countless lifeless bodies emerge from the ground. Although they were all half naked, there was nothing overtly erotic about their staging. None of the mannequins were posed directly next to each other in anything resembling a sex act. Instead, their posture suggested subservience, and, although their hands weren't arranged in prayer, there was something vaguely religious about the way they were positioned.

Hayden, who happened to be with us that night, was the first to act. He ran to the front door and knocked loudly. We quickly joined him to present a united front, but, as expected, no one answered. He knocked harder and yelled that it wasn't funny, but still no one answered. He yelled, "Why are you doing this?" and was met with silence. Hayden tried the front door but found it locked.

As we walked away, at least a couple of us claimed to hear strains of jazz music coming from the house. However, when we turned around and went back to the door, the music was gone. For several minutes we just stood there looking at the vast lawn and the collection of bodies on their knees. Eventually Hayden said, "We can't just leave them here like this." Everyone nodded, but no one moved yet. We were all too busy sizing up the logistics of the situation. There were fewer of us than there were mannequins, so we each had to take at least three. They didn't weigh too much, but it was difficult to carry three at once, so we ended up dragging them. As we made our way across the dewy grass, we were struck by just how much resistance we felt.

THE MEETING

The boys took turns guessing which man might be their daddy. Casey got to go first, and he pointed at a tall man wearing a dark gray suit, blue dress shirt, and matching tie. His black hair was full and had just a hint of wave to it. As the man walked out of the apartment building, he glanced at his gold watch.

"I betcha it's him," said Casey. "I bet he owns that whole building."

Lance jumped down from the monkey bars and shook his head.

"Naw," Lance said. "I bet it's him over there."

Lance was pointing to a guy sitting at a nearby park bench smoking a cigarette. The man wore a cutoff t-shirt and had tattoos all down his ropy looking arms. He wore a Detroit Tigers ball cap, some jean shorts, and white sneakers speckled with mud.

"I betcha he would take us to ballgames every week," Lance said. "Probably he'd even give us a sip of beer too."

Carla, their sister, laughed and shook her head.

"You two are nuts if you think we're gonna find our dad."

Carla didn't bother getting into the fact that the three of them didn't all have the same father. If they didn't know it now, then they would someday; and if they were too stupid to figure it out, then that was on them. All Carla knew for sure was they weren't up north in this tourist city looking for her daddy, because that fool had gotten himself locked up.

"Mama said dad called her and told us we should all move up here with him," Casey said. "She said he has a good job and big apartment for us all to live in."

Carla looked across the park at the apartment where their mom had told them to meet her. She had put the three of them up for a couple nights at a cheap motel and given Carla an address and a time to show up. It wasn't the first time their mom had done something like this, but usually she only left for one night at a time.

"She says a lot of things," Carla said. "And most of them ain't true."

Casey and Lance looked at each and frowned. They started to argue, but she cut them off by saying, "If you're so sure our dad's here, why don't you walk up to one of those guys and introduce yourself."

The boys looked at each other and then out at the park. The businessman had already walked away; but the other guy was still at the bench. He was looking at the distant bay, the cigarette still in his hands, burning close to his fingertips. He seemed to be concentrating on something, perhaps one of the sailboats out on the water. After a minute, he jumped up from the table and let the cigarette fall to the ground.

"Mother fucker!" the man said.

He stared back and forth between his fingers and the fallen cigarette like he didn't understand what had happened.

"I guess we'll just wait till ma gets back before we do anything," Lance said.

The park had filled up with mothers taking their children on a picnic. It was hot out, too. Earlier in the day, back when Carla had been more hopeful, she had been shivering in her tank-top and shorts. Now she was sweating like crazy even while sitting in the shade of the tall oaks at one corner of the park. Her brothers both probably had sunburns already, but they never seemed to care. Carla hated getting burnt. She didn't tan as well as her brothers; her skin was lighter and dotted with small freckles that most people didn't notice until they were real close. It was hard enough getting to sleep most nights anyway, but when she had a burn her clothes felt like sandpaper against her skin.

Even though she was in the shade now, the heat made her feel like she was getting too much sun.

She got up from where she was sitting and walked over to where Lance and Casey were throwing acorns at each other. After telling them to cut it out, she said they were going to get lunch.

"I thought you said we didn't have no money," Casey said.

"Yeah," Lance said. "When we asked to buy donuts you said we didn't have any."

Carla crossed her arms over her chest and said, "Do you two want to eat or not?" Without waiting for them to answer, she turned and started walking out of the park. They were sprinting within seconds. They raced out in front but fell in next to her as they came to the edge of the park.

"What time did mom say she would meet us?" Casey said.

"Yeah," Lance said. "And how will she know where to find us if we leave the park?"

She didn't know the answers to either of the questions. She felt lightheaded from the heat and her empty stomach, and she just wanted the boys to shut up for a second.

"You two can stay here if you want," she said. "But I'm going to get some food."

Carla swung her purse forward and held it against her stomach. The other hand she kept on her hip. This was a move her mom did all the time, and she hated that she had picked up on it somehow, but she kept doing it anyway. Carla didn't know what she hated more: how much she looked like their mom in this position or the fact that it brought her some comfort and made her feel in control of situations.

"Where are we going to eat?" both boys asked at once.

They ate at a diner a block away from the park. The place was full: lots of families, some old-timers at the counter. She chose a table near the back and told the boys not to make too much noise. "We're trying to keep a low profile." This was something her dad used to say. Carla had always enjoyed the secretive way he had said it; the emphasis on we made it seem like you and him were the only people in the world. Of course, he hadn't done too great a job of staying out of trouble.

It took the waitress several minutes to come by. The boys had already decided on hamburgers without seeing the menu and were now on to smashing salt and pepper shakers together. As the waitress approached, Carla elbowed Lance. The waitress was young, maybe only a couple years older than Carla. She seemed tired, and her limp, dull brown hair looked like it hadn't been washed in days. She took in the sight of the three of them and said, "I'll come back when your mom gets here."

"She is here," Carla said. "She's in the restroom and she told us to order even if she wasn't back."

The waitress narrowed her eyes and cocked her head.

"We've been out running errands all morning, and she needed a minute to fix herself up."

Before the waitress could say anything else, Carla rattled off their orders: hamburgers, French fries, and cokes for the three of them; and a club sandwich with a cup of soup for their mom. The girl wrote this all down on her pad of paper in sharp, noisy scribbles. Carla wondered if the waitress was actually writing their order.

"Oh yeah," Carla said. "Our mom wants a coffee, too. Black."

The waitress sighed and scribbled another word on the pad.

"Of course."

And then she was off into the bustle of the restaurant, people asking her for more ketchup, more coffee, more fries. More. Carla could relate. Lance and Casey always wanted something from her too: more time at the playground, more food, more candy. Even when their mom was around, the boys rarely asked of her what they asked of Carla. Probably because they knew mom wouldn't (or couldn't) get it, Carla thought.

Once the waitress was out of sight, Lance and Casey started up again about their dad.

"I bet he can hold his breath underwater for like two minutes."

"I bet he can swim across the whole bay."

She stopped listening after a minute and stared at the entrance of the restaurant. Even though it seemed unlikely, she kept hoping their mom would walk through the door. Carla could picture her face trying to cover the disappointment: the way she smiled without showing her teeth, lips pressed together like she was trying to force back tears. As much as she hated seeing that expression, Carla wouldn't have minded it right now.

The waitress came by a minute later with their drinks. She set them on the table quickly and left without saying a word. If the waitress remembered that their mom was supposed to join them, she didn't say anything. Lance and Casey grabbed for their cokes and took long drinks without putting their straws in. Carla put the straw in her own drink, had a sip, and started pushing the coffee toward the empty seat meant for their mom. But halfway through the motion she stopped and brought the coffee to her mouth: the smell of it was bitter and sharp. She took a cautious sip while forcing herself to look away from the entrance.

They ate their food quietly. The boys didn't even kick each other underneath the table or burp. The waitress came by once, asked how their food was without completely stopping, and then left the check. When the boys were finished, Carla told them to go wash up.

"And make sure to pee, too," she said.

Once they were out of sight, she stared at the check on the table. Without even opening her purse, she knew how much money was left: enough to cover the bill, but not much more. If she used it up, they wouldn't be able to buy another meal, only a snack. If she skipped out on the check, the waitress would probably have to pay their tab out of her own pocket. Carla remembered their mom complaining about customers like that back when she used to actually have a steady job. People like that should be shot. Carla tried not to think about this, or whether the waitress had a family or bills. She reached into her purse and grabbed a few dollars and a pen. The second she saw the boys coming back, she arranged the money as best as she could. Underneath the small pile, on the check, she wrote one word.

"Let's go," she told them.

They moved through the restaurant without making eye contact with anyone; they didn't look back either. Carla took slow breaths to keep her heart from speeding up too much. She pushed open the door, and the hot air outside felt like a blast from an oven. She kept walking, down the block, across the street, through the park, and up to the door of the apartment building. Lance and Casey walked beside her, heads down, mouths closed.

Carla stared at the address above the door until her eyes went blurry. They were the same numbers mom had given her. She knew this without rechecking the worn piece of paper with mom's messy handwriting. She looked over at the boys and thought of what mom had said to her before she had left. It was something like, Watch over them for me or Take real good care of them. Usually she just said, I love you or See you soon.

"Can we go in?" Casey said.

Carla tried to remember if she had seen anyone go in the building without using a key, but she couldn't. The heat was getting to her, and she was trying not to consider the possibility of having to tell her brothers the truth.

Before she could manage a response, Lance grabbed the door and pulled. It opened slowly.

"Sure," Carla said. "But we have to be quiet. We're trying to keep a low profile."

The halls of the apartment building were quiet. The carpet was a dark green, and the walls were an ugly beige. But it did seem clean, and it was for sure nicer than some of the places they had been, especially the motel where they'd just stayed: each of the two nights had been filled with people knocking on their door, and Carla had shoved a chair under the door handle in addition to keeping it locked, but she still hadn't been able to sleep.

"Which apartment is ours?" Lance said.

Carla thought for a moment about what she could say but decided to tell the truth.

"I don't know," she said.

She smiled and shrugged.

"I don't know," she said again, surprised by how good the truth can feel sometimes.

Then she came up with a plan of splitting up and listening at each door to see if they could hear her.

"Cool," Lance said. "It's kind of like a game."

"Sure," Carla said. "But we have to be quiet. If you talk or stomp around, you lose. Automatically."

The boys nodded.

"Can we pretend we're spies?" Casey said.

Carla shrugged a "why not" and told them to get going. But before they were out of sight, she said, "If there's any trouble, meet me back at the park." They both clenched their jaws and then walked up the stairs, their footsteps quieter than she'd ever heard them.

Left alone, she felt tired, and convinced that they were wasting their time. She wanted a place to lie down, a place where she could close her eyes and not worry about noises outside or where their mom was. Stay with it, she told herself. But even her inner voice sounded weak. She wished she had tasted more than one sip of the coffee back at the diner.

She put these thoughts aside and walked slowly through the hallway, until she came to the first door. With her shoulder and head leaning against the door, she listened for a solid minute without hearing anything. The same thing happened at the next one, and the one after that. At the fourth door, she heard something: a television. She couldn't hear it too well — either the walls were thick or the volume was low — but after listening for a while she could tell it was the news, which meant it probably wasn't mom. In her whole life, Carla couldn't ever remember her mom watch the news; her mom would change the channel and watch a commercial just to avoid seeing what was going on in the world. I don't see how knowing any of that could help me, she would say. Now that Carla was bit older, she wondered if her mom just had worried she'd end up on T.V. for some scam she had pulled.

Carla was about to cross the hallway and start on the other side, but she stopped and knocked on the door. Maybe whatever guy she was with liked the news. Within a few seconds, Carla heard someone getting up. Their footsteps seemed soft, and they weren't moving too quick. Carla still had time to walk away: she could easily slip down the hallway and go upstairs to find her brothers. She knew it was the right move, but she couldn't make herself do it. She couldn't even make herself think of a response for whoever came to the door.

When the door opened, a blast of cold air came out. Carla shivered once, but it felt good. A lady dressed in jeans and a black sweater stood there smiling and holding a TV guide. She was older than Carla's mom, but not by a lot. Her gray-black hair probably made her seem older.

"Can I help you with something?" the woman said.

Carla told the truth again.

"I'm looking for someone that recently moved in here."

She proceeded to give the best description she could think of on the spot: tall, dyed blonde hair, and low-cut clothes. When the lady just stood there staring, Carla added one more detail: "She's very lonely."

The woman sighed.

"That," she said, clutching the T.V. guide to her chest, "describes a lot of the women who come through this place."

Carla couldn't find Lance and Casey upstairs. Her first instinct was to run for the park, but something made her wait and listen at each door for a split second. The first few were quiet, but at the fourth one she heard voices that sounded like her brothers. She tried the handle; it was unlocked, so she went in. This apartment felt hot and smelled like cigarettes and stale fried chicken; the smell made her stomach flip, but it did remind her of half the places she'd ever lived.

Right away she saw Lance and Casey sitting on a couch. They were leaning over a coffee table playing cards. A man she didn't recognize sat in a chair across the table from them.

"Go fish," the man said.

Casey smiled and reached for one of the cards. The man looked at Carla as she walked over to the couch and gave each of her brothers a little smack on the wrist. They both frowned and said ouch.

"You were supposed to find me before you went anywhere," she said. "You scared the shit out of me."

The man smiled and told her it was O.K. He had a wide smile, but one side was pinched like he had a mouthful of chew.

"Yeah," Lance said. "He's our daddy."

That's what he told you, but it doesn't mean it's true, she thought. But even as she said this, she couldn't help noticing Lance and Casey did look a lot like him.

"What else did he tell you?" Carla said.

"He said even though he's our dad we could just call him Pete if we wanted," Casey said.

Carla nodded and watched while Lance put down a pair of eights on the table.

"Pete," she said. "Could I talk to you in the kitchen for a second?"

In the kitchen, Pete offered her a seat at a small table cluttered with an ashtray, newspapers, dirty dishes, and matchbooks from different bars. When she waved this off, he asked if she wanted a cigarette.

"You look old enough for that," he said, more to himself than anything else.

Carla had smoked before — usually cigarettes swiped from her mom — but she wasn't quite old enough by law. The fact that this Pete guy didn't know this said a lot.

"No thanks," she told him.

He shrugged and lit himself a cigarette with a match from one of the matchbooks. On the inside cover she noticed someone had written several phone numbers.

"What have you already told them?" she said.

He flipped the matchbook closed, set it on the table, and looked right at her.

"Everything I told them is true."

He stared right at her, his lips together but relaxed. He wouldn't look away or blink, and it reminded her of the stare-down contests Lance and Casey would have. Cigarette smoke rose between them, making her eyes water.

"Okay," she said, blinking. "I believe you. Now tell me where my mom is."

Pete sighed and took a long drag off his cigarette. He still hadn't blinked yet, and it was making her uneasy.

"I don't know," he said, finally blinking. He crushed his cigarette in the ashtray even though it was only half gone. "I wrote her after I got out of jail and told her she should bring the boys up north here. Part of me didn't think she'd actually make it, but then one day she showed up. Things were pretty good at first until I let slip I didn't have a job yet."

Pete shook his head and looked down at the table. He moved around some of the matchbooks like they were puzzle pieces.

"She freaked out, didn't she?" Carla said.

Pete nodded.

"She hit me a couple times while screaming that I was a liar. When she stopped yelling, she locked herself in the room and cried. I tried explaining that I had a good job lined up that started next month, but she wouldn't listen. I even told her I had enough money to last all of us until the job started. Once she heard that, she stopped crying and started going through all my shit. I could hear her opening up drawers and moving stuff around in there ..."

Pete quit moving the matchbooks around and slammed his fist on the table. The noise made her jump.

"I could give her a decent life, you know," he said, his eyes squinted like there was still smoke close. "I could give all of you a decent life."

She made herself look him in the eye instead of at his fist on the table. When he started to tear up, she made herself look away.

Pete let them know they could stay as long as they wanted. "She'll probably be back tomorrow," he said. They were all back in the living room now. The boys had given up on Go Fish, leaving the cards scattered all over the coffee table. They stared out the main window, which had a partial view of the water. Even though sunset wasn't for another couple hours, there was a resigned, cluttered feeling to the room that Carla associated with the end of a day.

"You two would like staying here, right?" Pete said.

The boys said "Sure" without turning to look at Pete. Right away Carla thought of what their mom had said about staying over places. Never stay alone with any man, unless it's your dad. She tried not to picture the men their mom had been with since dad was locked up, tried not to hear what went on behind the closed doors.

"What about you?" he said to Carla.

Lance and Casey turned to look at her. They both seemed hopeful: they smiled and raised their eyebrows. Carla nodded but crossed her fingers behind her back, hoping the boys would see.

"Good," Pete said. "There's plenty of room here. I'm going to fix myself a drink, and then we can go swimming. There's a beach a few minutes away from here."

Once he was out of the room, Carla gathered the boys close to her and started whispering. She told them they weren't staying the night with a man they didn't know, even if he was their father. "Mom's rules," she said, before they could do any complaining.

From the kitchen, Carla heard the sound of ice hitting a glass. The boys stood there with their mouths open.

"We'll wait till he's in the bathroom, and then we'll leave."

They both shook their heads; Lance quietly asked if she could let go of their wrists.

"Yeah," Casey whispered. "You're hurting us."

Carla looked down and released her grip; their wrists were red and scratched from where her fingernails had dug in.

"Fine," she said. "Be stupid if you want. But I can't stay here knowing mom's out there somewhere."

Pete came back out to the living room with a drink in one hand and a cigarette in the other. The drink was half gone already. He looked happier now but also tired.

"You guys have swimsuits with you?" he said.

Carla frowned and said, "You see our suitcases anywhere?" Casey spoke up and said all their stuff was in a locker at the bus station. Carla felt the familiar prick of shame when she thought about all their belongings stuffed in a cheap duffel bag. Even though she knew the key was still in her pocket, she checked for it anyway. It was still there, and so was the key to the motel room where they had been staying: she must've forgotten to turn it in when they left.

Pete laughed and said they could just swim in their shorts.

"Yeah," Lance said. "We do it all the time."

Carla thought about saying, No, you do it all the time. I'm a girl. I can't swim in my shorts and tank top. But she didn't. Making a scene now wouldn't do any good. She had missed her chance the other day when she had let their mom walk out on them.

"Sure," she said. "I guess I'm up for it."

The beach was crowded. Only a few people were swimming, but the adjoining park was filled with people barbequing and milling about. It seemed like they were all part of one group, and near as she could tell, it was some local church or mission sponsoring a dinner for the homeless: half the people wore layers of oversized clothes and smelled like they hadn't bathed in a week, while the other half wore crisp short sleeved white button up shirts and khakis. None of the people seemed dressed for the beach.

Lance and Casey didn't seem to notice anything besides the water. They ran right in, stopping only to peel off their t-shirts and throw them in the direction of the towels Pete had brought. Pete had chosen a spot that was directly in the sun, but Carla had asked if they could move.

"I burn pretty easy," she said, and pointed to a few scrubby trees down the way.

He picked up the towels and followed her over. He wore a swimsuit but didn't seem to be in a hurry to get in. After stretching out on a towel, he lit a cigarette and looked out at the boys playing in the water.

"You sure you don't want to swim?" he said. "There's a drugstore a couple blocks away, and I think they might sell bathing suits."

She told him no thanks. He turned to her and smiled before looking back at the boys.

"You seem all right," she said.

The words had tumbled out without her thinking about them. He took a long drag from his cigarette and scratched his chin.

"I guess so," he said.

"Do you really think Casey and Lance are yours?"

Without any hesitation, he turned to her and laughed.

"You think I would offer to take in a bunch of kids when I got barely any money and no job unless they were my own?"

She considered this for a moment while she watched Lance and Casey play some form of water tag with another kid about their age. Near as she could tell, you were safe as long as you could stay underwater, and a side goal of the game seemed to be making a big splash when you went under.

"I guess not," she said, without looking at Pete.

She waited for him to say something more, but he seemed to have lost interest in the conversation: he was looking at the homeless people and the barbeque. She closed her eyes for a moment and pictured her dad's face, the hard blue eyes that softened when they looked at her or her mom, the scar on his left cheek, the way he moved his chin and jaw slightly when he got nervous. What would he think about her hanging around some guy who claimed to be the boys' father?

"I'm going to get some barbeque," Pete said. "You want anything?"

She knew it was stupid to turn down free food, but she didn't feel like anything right now.

"Maybe a drink," she said. "Some water or some lemonade."

Pete nodded and walked toward the picnic tables. Carla watched him for a moment then turned her attention toward the boys. They were still playing tag. There was almost no wind, so their laughter carried across the water and sand to where she was. She couldn't imagine how their mom could walk away from all of them. If she ever stopped to picture their faces or hear their voices, their laughter, then she'd for sure come back.

Carla repeated this idea so many times that she became convinced something had happened to their mom. Maybe she was in jail, or maybe some drug dealer had her locked up in an apartment somewhere. She should've realized this and gone looking for her a long time ago, and the fact that she hadn't sickened her. She stood up from the towel, turned her back to the water, and started walking.

As she walked off the beach, she made plans for all the places she could check. She moved slowly, knowing full well that any minute a voice would call her back. And, like all the other times that mattered, she knew she would do as she was told.

John Abbott

THE SWEETEST BOY I KNOW

Leo Strattan sat by the drafty second story window waiting for his mom to return home from her date. Despite repeated questioning she refused to tell her son who the man was. "You'll like him," she had said. "You two have a lot in common." To kill time and distract himself he scanned the apartment section of the Kalamazoo Gazette for places he could afford. It was no good being twenty years old and still living with his mom, even though he did it for her benefit. With a black permanent marker he circled ones with potential and slashed x's across ones that were too expensive. He didn't set down the paper until it looked like one big tic tac toe board. He had been repeating this ritual for two years now, ever since he graduated high school. In that time he had circled plenty of rentals but had never called on any of them.

Leo jolted awake in his chair when he heard the front door of the building swing open with creaking hinges and an accompanying gust of wind. He didn't know how long he had slept for. The last detail he remembered was watching snow fall by the glow of the streetlight outside the window. He stood up, letting the newspaper fall from his lap. He blinked twice and rubbed his eyes before walking through his front door and into the hallway. The building's hallway reminded him of an old hotel with its worn shag carpet, chandeliers, and faded yellowish gold wallpaper. It smelled like old newspapers because the downstairs neighbor collected them in twine wrapped bundles that nearly blocked her door. He crouched down and peered over the dark wood banister at the person walking in but he could tell by the hair it wasn't his mom. After he realized this he stood up.

The woman raised her head and he recognized Sadie, a young college student roughly his age, who lived in the apartment next door. They were friends, maybe more.

157

He had gone out with her a couple times, usually to a movie or the coffee shop down the street. Each time they ended up at her place afterwards, on the cold-to-the-touch leather couch where they'd make out for a while. But during this span of a month or so Leo had seen her with other guys, several times, though he never mentioned it to her.

She smiled up at him as she took off her charcoal gray scarf and black gloves. Snowflakes melted and dripped down from strands of her raven black curly hair. She was an exceptionally pretty girl, tall with lithe arms that seemed like they belonged to a dancer. Her face wore a habitual impish expression brought out by the contrast between her wide smile and her tiny nose.

In a nasally Midwestern accent she asked Leo what he was doing in the hallway. He told her he was waiting up for his mom.

"Do you wait up for your mom every night?" she asked.

"Only when she's out on a date," he said.

She laughed at his response and Leo wondered if she thought he was joking. She headed up the steps, leaving a trail of snowy footprints on the carpet. Outside her door she unlaced her boots halfway down and then yanked and tugged at them as if they were choking the life out of her feet. At one point she almost toppled over and had to brace herself against the wall. Her cheeks were flushed from the cold and all puffed out from the exertion of taking off her boots. Leo tried, but couldn't quite manage to stop himself from laughing.

"I knew I shouldn't have bought this pair," she said.

"Why didn't you just undo all the laces?" he asked.

"Probably because I'm lazy," she said as she finally got out of her boots. "So is your mom really on a date?" she asked.

He nodded.

"And you're staying up till she gets home?"

He nodded again and started to prepare an explanation for her but she cut him off.

"Then why don't you come over to my place for a drink? You'll still be able to hear her when she gets back."

"That sounds nice," he said.

"What would you like to drink?" she asked once they were inside.

"Whatever you're having."

He took a seat on the familiar leather couch while she went to the kitchen. It always felt strange sitting in this apartment that was at once identical to his own and completely different. Both featured nice hardwood floors and beautiful arched entryways leading from the living room to the dining room. Much of the paint was peeling and water stains blotched the wall where it met the ceiling. The old radiator underneath the windowsill occasionally sputtered and gasped like it was pleading for someone to end its misery. But when it came to the decorating, the two apartments seemed like different worlds. Sadie's furniture looked expensive and new compared to the thrift store bargains he and his mom owned. And her walls were covered with framed Salvador Dali prints and posters of rock and roll bands. Only a tacky pastoral painting graced his walls.

After a couple of minutes she returned with two glasses of red wine. She handed one to him before sitting down on the couch.

"Are you cold?" she asked. "The heat doesn't work too well but I could get you a blanket."

"I'll be fine. The heat doesn't work well at my place either so I'm used to it," he said.

"You want to know a secret?" she asked.

She curled her feet under her behind and leaned toward him like she was really going to whisper in his ear. He could smell her perfume, something sweet and fresh that reminded him of honeysuckle.

"Sometimes I drink a whole bottle of wine just to stay warm," she said. "That's bad isn't it?"

"No, it's not bad."

Leo didn't drink too often and when he did he never had more than two or three drinks, but it wasn't because he took any moral stand against it or even because his father, when his parents were still together, drank too much and hit his mother. His reason was simply that he didn't have much experience with it and he hated having no idea how he would act after several drinks. He took a sip from his glass. He didn't know good wine from bad but nevertheless told her he liked it.

"Thanks," she said as she drank some from her glass. "I wasn't going to but I have to ask why you stay up till your mom gets home?"

His first thought was to say that she needed taking care of but he didn't want to sound like some jerk who thinks women need men to protect them. At the same time he didn't want to bore her with details from his mom's past.

"I don't know the guy she went out with and until I do I just feel kind of uncomfortable."

"I think it's sweet of you," she said. "Not many guys would do that."

"Thanks," he said.

Other women had told Leo how sweet he was but it never helped him feel better about the situation. It didn't ease the embarrassment when he had to bail his mom out of jail when she got arrested for public indecency. It didn't take away the shame he felt when he was too young to protect his mom from his father. Whenever someone called him sweet he thought of Marjorie Ellsworth. He had dated her for a few months in high school until she broke up with him, not to his face, but in a letter. She had ended the relationship because he moved too slow. He didn't even kiss her till they had gone out for a month. He didn't touch her breasts until she placed his fingertips on her swollen light brown nipples. They never had sex. His hesitance in the physical realm of their relationship had its roots from seeing the way men treated his mom as nothing more than a sexual object. That, plus the memories, both distant and recent, of hearing her mom and whatever guy she had brought home having sex in the next room caused Leo to wilt whenever he got to a certain point with women.

The only part of Marjorie's letter he remembered was the last line, which read, and I'm really sorry to do this to you because you really are the sweetest boy I know. Even though he burned the letter after reading it, he still felt the same prickle of embarrassment on his face when he recalled those words.

They sat in silence for a few minutes while they both finished their wine. He enjoyed her company very much; even when they weren't speaking, it didn't feel uncomfortable. He tried to keep his mind off his mom and her date. Besides, she usually stayed out till two o'clock when the bars closed and it was only eleven right now.

"I'm going to have another glass," she said. "Do you want one?"

He nodded. When she left again he studied the posters on the wall. Most of the band names didn't mean anything to him. Maybe he'd ask her about them. He realized that he knew very little about Sadie. Their dates, or whatever they were, usually didn't involve much talking. Really all he knew was that she came from Chicago to Kalamazoo to study psychology at Western Michigan University.

When she returned, he asked her some questions about school. He listened to her talk about which psychological disorders interested her most but mainly he watched the way she gestured with her hands while she spoke. She extended the hand which held the wine glass out and away from her body in quick energized motions as if to punctuate her sentences. The glass was close to full and the deep red liquid sloshed close to the rim each time but didn't spill, although he expected it to.

Sadie was in the middle of describing a woman that she knew who had a multiple personality disorder when she set her glass down and touched Leo's wrist.

"This is going well, don't you think," she said.

"What is?"

"Us having a drink. Do you think we should consider this our first date?" as she spoke her voice rose to an excited pitch.

Leo set his glass on the coffee table alongside hers. He kissed her and they fell back onto the pillows. Her mouth tasted fruity like the wine and he pulled away only to get closer to her intoxicating smell. He pressed his nose into the warmth of her neck where the scent was strongest. While he bit and licked there, he trailed his hand down her body where he unbuttoned her jeans. His hand paused, as if by reflex, on the warm cotton of her underwear. He had expected his hand to be trembling by now, like it always did, but it held steady. This shocked him and he wondered if the wine had maybe loosened him up. Flush, both in his face and groin, he lifted her waistband. His fingers trailed through bristly hair and rested on her sex. Without any conscious effort on his part, the unwelcome sounds of his mom's lovemaking, the moans and the headboard thumping rhythmically against the wall, flooded his mind. He wanted very much to continue but he didn't see any way he could now. But then he remembered something that he had heard when he moved into the building a couple months ago.

On that first night Leo had lain awake in bed acclimating himself to the new sounds of his apartment. Just before sleep came to him, he heard a woman's voice. At first he thought it was his mom but then he realized the sound had filtered through the cheaply made wall that separated his apartment from the one next door. He listened closer and quickly understood he was hearing people having sex. He focused on the woman's passionate cries and, though he felt guilty about his voyeurism, took care of his erection. He didn't know it then, but the woman was his neighbor Sadie.

It didn't take much effort for that memory to replace the ones of his mom. The pleasure of knowing he could make her sound that way again increased Leo's desire so much that he felt feverish. Without any more hesitation he touched her with an urgency that pleasantly surprised both of them. It was as if, through his unbounded enthusiasm, he was making up for all the times he should have done this but didn't.

He pulled away from her when he heard the front door of the building open then slam shut so hard the pictures on her wall shook.

"Why are you stopping?" she asked.

"That might be my mom," he said.

"She's home now so it's OK," she said. "Please keep touching me," she said as she slid her jeans and underwear down so he might have better access.

A voice from downstairs bellowed out a stream of what sounded to Leo like curses. He rushed to the door and stepped into the hallway. He made it to the top of the staircase before Sadie had pulled up and buttoned her pants.

"You haven't changed one bit," the man said. "You're still a cheap fucking whore. Can't keep your hands off any guy who buys you a drink."

From where Leo stood he couldn't see the man's face, only the back of his head. The man faced his mom with one hand held up, fingers splayed, and slapped her. His fingers left red imprints on her milky complexion. She looked up the stairs and saw her son. She blinked twice as if she didn't believe it was him and then she mouthed his name. Leo ran downstairs. The man startled at the noise and turned around. Although Leo hadn't seen him in ten years he knew it was his dad. Aside from the obvious age difference the two looked almost identical. They had the same brown eyes, olive skin, and heaviness in the jaw.

"What do you think you're gonna do?" his dad said. The sharp smell of vodka filled the air and spittle formed at the corners of his mouth as he spoke. "I bet you're still the same pussy you were ten years ago."

As he prepared to defend his mom he couldn't help but wonder if his dad still carried his old Swiss army knife. The same knife he cut mom with. He never could shake the memory of that night. He had awoken to his mom's scream and ran to their bedroom where he saw the whole scene unfold. His mom wore only a sheer white slip and his dad had on boxers, his erection visible as it prodded against the checkered blue and red material. The smell of their sex hung in the air but at the time Leo mistook it as the stench of fear. Dad stood in a square of moonlight and the shadow of the knife's curved blade seemed to stretch forever. He never understood where he got the knife from since they were both practically naked. All he could think of was that dad slept with it underneath his pillow.

He brought the blade to where her cleavage showed above her slip and angled it down. Leo thought he meant to hack off her breast but he ran the flat part of the knife over the curve and let it rest on her nipple. Then in one swift motion he skimmed it across the skin on her collarbone. The blood spilled from the cut and dripped onto her slip. Until that moment neither his mom nor dad knew he was standing there; but he gasped when he saw blood and gave himself away. His dad charged out of the room and shoved the knife in front of his face. "You want some of this you little shit?" he said and then pushed him to the ground. He lay on the carpet shaking his head no but his dad didn't see because he had gone back to the bedroom for some clothes before he left the house. To this day he didn't understand, and maybe didn't want to, what words or actions could have interrupted their lovemaking and prompted his dad to pull out a knife.

Leo held onto the image of his mom bleeding onto her white slip as he hit his dad in the nose. He swung again and again, each time connecting with stubbly flesh. When he fell to the floor Leo stood above him and continued to pummel his face even though his hands ached and were sticky with blood. He heard a voice yelling his name but it wasn't his mom because she was standing right in front of him. He turned to see Sadie coming down the stairs.

"Leo, you're going to hurt him," Sadie said.

"He's my dad," he said this as if she knew all the horrible things the man had done. "He hit her just now. I had to do something."

She nodded her head.

"He cut her too," Leo said. "That's why she always wears those scarves," he pointed to his mom whose face was still frozen in surprise. She turned to them at the mention of the scarf and walked over to Leo's side.

"I didn't try to stop him," Leo said. "He probably would have killed me if I tried."

As he spoke he realized he had never told anyone these stories before and here he was telling a girl he barely knew. He hoped that all this drama wouldn't freak her out so much that she wouldn't see him again. If that happened, he told himself, he'd move out and leave his mom to fend for herself. He would feel terrible, of course, but it might teach her a lesson.

"Why are you telling her all these things Leo?" his mom asked as she fidgeted with her scarf. "Are you trying to embarrass me?"

He really wanted to tell her to shut her damn mouth for once but he knew there was no point. She'd just get even more unruly and start lecturing about how much she had sacrificed for him. If he tried to say anything back to her she'd yell so loud it'd wake up everyone in the building and in the morning she wouldn't remember any of what happened. She wouldn't understand why the neighbors looked at her funny when they passed her in the hall.

Leo opened his mouth to apologize to her but before he could he heard a raspy wheeze no louder than a whisper from behind him. He didn't understand the words so he turned around and at the same time he felt the searing pain of the knife entering his left ankle. He jumped back and the handle slipped out of his dad's hand; but the blade remained in Leo's leg. Derrick Strattan smiled and moved his lips, causing a pinkish bubble of blood to pop. He pressed his palms flat on the ground and tried to stand but fell back on his chest.

Leo's mom yelled hysterically and Sadie tried to calm her down but Leo didn't pay any attention to them. He kicked his dad with his right foot and watched the smile disappear. He bent down to yank the knife from his ankle. The blood gushed out faster but he didn't try to stop its flow. He knelt on the ground to make sure his dad was unconscious and as a mixture of blood and alcohol hit his nose he tried to remember something good, or at least something not violent, about his dad. His mind flashed back to the time mom lectured dad, a rare event in their family, one morning at breakfast about never being there for his son.

"Every night you work late and then come home drunk after Leo's already asleep," she said. "It's like he doesn't even have a father."

Leo looked down at his plate of runny eggs and burnt toast. He tensed up as he waited for the sound of dad hitting her but it didn't come. Derrick leveled his finger at her and said, "You have no right to say that. Our son is lucky to have me around. I had no one. No father. No mother. No brothers or sisters. I didn't have anyone who gave two shits about me."

Afterwards they all sat in silence. Leo, not wanting to upset his parents by leaving food on his plate, scooped the rest of his lukewarm eggs onto the toast and shoveled it into his mouth. As he chewed, some of the yolk dribbled onto his chin. His dad sipped at his coffee but didn't touch the rest of his food. Later that day Derrick took his son to the park and pushed him on the swings. It was a cold Saturday in late October and the park was empty except for a couple bums sleeping on benches. The wind blew away the newspaper they used as blankets and it seemed to cut right through the jean jacket Leo wore. He couldn't feel his fingertips where they gripped the steel links on the swing's handles but he didn't ask to go home. His dad kept pushing him higher, higher than he had ever gone before, so that each time he thought for sure the swing would wrap around the steel beam at the top and he'd fly off; but he never did. After a while he had to shut his eyes because the gusts of wind made his eyes water and this left him free to focus on the sensation of flying that was only interrupted briefly by his dad's hands on his back.

The next Saturday he waited patiently all morning for his dad to wake up, all the while hoping that they would go to the park again. At noon his mom informed him that dad hadn't come home last night. It was the first time, that Leo knew of, he slept somewhere else.

"We should get you to the hospital," Sadie said. "Let me get my coat and I'll drive you."

Leo sat down on the steps while she went upstairs. His ankle throbbed with pain but it seemed manageable as long as he didn't have to put pressure on it.

"What are we going to do about your dad?" his mom asked. "You can't leave me here alone with him."

He couldn't believe her. She still expected her son to take care of her even though she had gotten herself into this situation. He almost asked her what the hell she had in mind when she went out with his dad but that would be like asking why she dated any of the losers she did over the last ten years. Her response would always be the same lie, "I think it would be good for you to have a male role model."

"Go upstairs and lock yourself in the apartment. Then call the police," he said.

She backed her way up the stairs, one hand on the banister, and fixed her wide-eyed stare on Derrick like he might suddenly spring to his feet and run after her. Leo heard the deadbolt snap shut and closed his eyes. He listened to the hum of the chandelier above him and the much louder sound of the wind outside. He fixed his attention on the noises to distract himself from the pain in his ankle. With each gust of wind, Leo's mind seemed to drift farther away from reality. He used to do this as a child whenever he couldn't deal with his parents. Like many children, he thought that if he thought real hard the sheer power of his will might transport him somewhere else. But when he opened his eyes, this time he felt no disappointment, only a strange, detached calm that he didn't fully understand.

He brought his hand up to brush some hair from his eyes and in so doing he smelled Sadie on his fingers, a scent so primal that it brought back his erection with such force, it made him ache. As he sat and waited for Sadie to come back downstairs, only one thought occupied his head. He hoped that his injury wouldn't be too serious that it stood in the way of his coming home from the hospital tonight with Sadie so they could finish what they started. And, unless she asked, he wouldn't mention he had just lost his virginity.

ABOUT JOHN ABBOTT

Abbott is a writer, musician, and English instructor who lives with his wife and daughter in Kalamazoo, Michigan. His work has appeared or is forthcoming in *Redivider, The Potomac Review, Georgetown Review, Hawaii Pacific Review, Arcadia, Two Thirds North, upstreet, Bitter Oleander* and many others. His first novel *The Last Refrain* is now available from Sweatshoppe Publications, and his poetry chapbook *Near Harmony* is available from Flutter Press. For more information about his writing, please visit www.johnabbottauthor.com

John Abbott